Paper in the Wind
A Princess Lilly Story

Heidi E. McKearney

Dedication

For Oliver, Tino, Clyde, Pierre, Baxter, Gizzy and Pearl...
Your paw prints will remain, forever in my heart.

Contents

Dedication ii

Acknowledgements vi

Prologue ix

1 New Beginnings... 1

2 A New Adventure Awaits 8

3 The Connection 14

4 Monkey See Monkey Do 18

5 Leap of Faith 20

6 Searching for Lilly 24

7 A Close Call 27

8 Pep Talk 31

9 Chaos on the Main 36

10 School Daze 43

11 Play Ball 45

12 On the Road Again 61

13 Cats Meet Dog 64

14 Clear the Gym 69

15 Engine One Ladder Two 74

16 Cats to the "Rescue" 78

17 Schools Out 83

18 Back at the Ranch 89

19 Coffee and Donuts 90

20 The Reunion 94

21 End of the Road 108

22 The Balloon 114

23 On the Run 117

24 Up and Away... 122

25 All Hands on Deck 124

26 Sending Out an SOS_127

27 The Bus Stops Here 142

Acknowledgements

I'd like to extend my deepest gratitude to Lindsay Teixeira, graphic designer, and owner of, needleanddesign.com Without her adroit designing skills, patience, and dedication to this book writing project, my dream of publishing, Paper In The Wind, would not have come to fruition. My heartfelt thanks to my family, and friends, for their continued support, and patience, as this writing endeavor took longer than anticipated. An abundance of love, and special thanks to my grandchildren, Jade, Cody, Marlee, and Charlie, for inspiring the roles portrayed in this story. Jade, and Cody, complimented each other well, as they embarked upon a wild, and make-believe adventure together. And to Marlee, and Charlie, their role may have been small, but they're big in my heart, and I can envision them starring in an adventure story of their own, one day. Additionally, it is with great pride, that I commend my sons, Corey, and Jeremy, along with Jaquilina, and Christina, for raising such wonderful children. It is with the utmost adoration, I give thanks to all four of my sons, for being my driving force, each and every day. And so, to Corey, Jeremy, Brenden, and Elliot, I love you with all my heart. Finally, to my Heavenly Father, I give thanks for guiding my spirit, and answered prayers.

Prologue

Standing behind the gate, the wheelchair-bound dog, focused her gaze. Noticing the children gathered across the street, a protective instinct warned that something was amiss. Determined to know more, her pricked ears turned to listen, as an oppressive vibe spread across the bus-stop. Finally, pushing her nose through the chain-link fence, she worked to absorb all that she could through her superior olfactory. Then without warning, violence ensued, and she bore witness to an atrocity, never to be forgotten. Moments later, the school- bus arrived, and all climbed aboard, leaving behind a heart-wrenching scene. It was then, a strong determination prevailed to protect the broken and afraid, as the little brown dog dubbed, Princess Lilly, began to devise her bold, and heroic plan...

1 New Beginnings...

WITH A NEW LIFE IN Boston, came the promise of a safe and loving home. Lilly was a long way from her birthplace in Thailand. Leaving behind a treacherous life in Bangkok, she was no longer prone to sickness, hunger and a host of prevailing dangers that life on the streets would behold. Beating the odds, the young pup ultimately survived the greatest threat of all, as dog-meat smugglers prowled the city streets, determined to trap their unsuspecting victims. Destined for slaughter, Lilly found herself caged aboard a truck, ill-fated for human consumption. Clinging to life, her nightmarish reality became more than she could bear. In the end, a bittersweet rescue left her alive, but orphaned, never to see her biological mother and siblings again. In time, the broken-hearted pup allowed herself to love again in a newly adoptive home in Boston with four other rescue dogs. Adjusting to an unfamiliar lifestyle, Lilly spent her days enjoying a quiet life with Pierre, Oliver, Clyde and Tino, all dogs like she, who once upon a time found themselves lost and alone without a family to call their own. The four of them were content to dozing in the sunny corners of the backyard, but it was Lilly who kept her eye on a more audacious goal. Although small in stature, she maintained an enormous appetite for grand adventures that would forever motivate her to act upon her daredevil ideas...

With the start of each day, Lilly and her brothers routinely nosed around the modest confines of their backyard, delighting in an exploration of scents the nighttime left behind. Watching this, it warmed Heidi's heart to bear witness to her senior pack's enjoyment, as their peaceful contentment was her pleasure. But little did she know, the wheelchair-bound dog she dubbed, Princess Lilly, was up to no good, and was planning a mischievous getaway... Standing behind the gate, Lilly kept a curious eye on the school-bus as it rolled to a stop. Her pricked ears turned to the sound of the cheery group sporting their backpacks and sneakers, as they climbed aboard the bright yellow motor-coach and took their seats. Focusing her attention on the idling bus, it was then, Lilly began to devise her sneaky plan... Pierre knew better than to underestimate his sister's determination. "Lilly, I hope you're not thinking, what it is that I think you're thinking." he said, giving her a look. Curls of black framed his teddy-bear face, lending him an essence of pure innocence. It was plain to see, Lilly was contemplating a daring move, and for that, Pierre grew anxious. Looking to her brother, she played it down, hoping to put his worried mind at ease. "Just relax, Poodle. I'm just wondering about a few things, that's all." she said. "That's what I'm afraid of, Lilly. Once you get an idea in that head of yours, there's no telling what you might do." Pierre said, giving her a look. "So, where do you think they go every day?" Lilly asked, referring to the kids, boarding the bus. "Well, I just assumed they rode to school. Why do you ask?" Pierre questioned, puzzled by his sister's intrigue. "No reason, really. I'm just curious." she answered, but Pierre knew better than to trust in her vague answer, as the sneaky gleam in her eye spoke volumes.

As a dog of good nature, Pierre appreciated the simpler things in life. For it was the long walks, and time spent with his former person, that stood out, in the old dog's memory. A sweet companionship it was, until the sudden passing of the only person he ever truly loved. Alas, Pierre found himself locked behind the walls of the city pound, alone and afraid. And so, it became a day, filled with unbearable sadness, and confusion, for the newly orphaned dog. He tried to remain strong, and never gave up hope, and in time, he was lovingly, adopted into his present home. Bittersweet it was, as memories of his former person would always remain. Pierre believed that the true essence of love, was not fleeting or disposable, but everlasting in the heart for those we cared deeply. And the most cherished of all gifts, did not come bound in ribbons and bows, as it was the intangible treasures kept stowed in the heart, that were more valuable than silver or gold.

Before long, Oliver joined Lilly, and Pierre at the gate. Like Pierre, he knew his sister well, and shuddered to think what sneaky scheme, she might be plotting. Looking to the others, streaks of silvery, gray, streamed throughout his long, silky coat, suggestive of his senior years. Leaving behind a life in Thailand, he was finally, free to live out his golden years in the comforts of his newly adoptive home. Remembering his abandonment, Oliver was prone to danger, as his eyesight was limited, and he was forced to fend for himself in a volatile place with hundreds of others, all like he, who fought for food and dominance. Barely surviving attacks from other dogs, it was decided for his own protection, to cage him twenty-four hours a day, seven days a week. This cruel act, added to Oliver's life of misery, and fast became a sad existence of unbearable loneliness and isolation for years on end. With no human contact, he was starved for affection, and his nightmarish existence became one of unimaginable sadness and solitary confinement. But a merciful rescue and adoption, freed him from all that, and only then, was he able to experience a peaceful life, filled with love in his present home.

Padding his way across the yard, Clyde joined the others by the fence. Looking through the gate, his wide-eyed expression, hid behind long strands of silvery hair, draping his flat nose and chin. Much like Pierre, Clyde enjoyed his daily walks, but for the aging shih tzu, snacking was more his simple pleasure, and over time, began to show on his ever-increasing waistline. Like the others, he left behind a life of sadness, as his days were once filled with bitter loneliness at the local dog-pound. Left there by his former person, he tried to understand his abandonment, as he sat alone, trembling with fear. Clyde hoped to one day, return home, but sadly, that day never came. And so, he resigned to spending the final days of his life, in a place, where the dreams of a dog, faded like the wind.

Feeling worthless, Clyde believed that nobody would ever want a dog as aged as he. Bitter sadness filled his lonely heart, as he bore witness to others passing through the shelter doors, on their way to a better life. Clyde desperately wanted a chance at that too, but drained of all hope, he gave up on his only wish of finding a place, fit to call home. Then one fateful day when he least expected it, his condemned future took on a hopeful outlook. As he lay curled on his mat, his head perked at the sight of a woman, standing at his kennel door... He listened intently as she read aloud the sign, hanging on the gate... *Owner surrendered, adult male with heart condition and senior cataracts. Requires daily meds and eye drops...* The damming words left him feeling as though, nobody would ever want him. Clyde conceded to his homelessness, and hoped for nothing more, than the dank confines of the local dog-pound. But to his utter surprise, he took his freedom-walk that day, when the person who stood before his kennel door, recognized his loving potential, and opened her home, and heart to the dog who needed her most.

Tino was the elder of the group. As a teacup-size poodle, he wore a coat of pure white. Ringlets of soft fur, hugged his slight frame, lending him a soft cottony look, while tear-stains streaming from the corners of his eyes, contrasted against his snow-white appearance. Cataracts compromised his ability to see, but nothing could get past the old dog's superior sense of smell. Not so long ago, he too, found himself homeless, aimlessly wandering the city streets. Plagued with hunger, his malnourished body was reduced to nothing more than skin and bones. The odds were against the aging, pint-sized poodle, as blindness put him at a greater risk to the many dangers a bustling city could behold. But as luck would have it, Tino wound up, at the same city pound as Clyde. So, on the fateful day that Clyde took his freedom walk, Tino, did too...

With everyone gathered by the gate, Lilly confessed her daring plan. Judging by her brother's worried looks, she knew, gaining their approval would take some doing. "Come on, you guys... Where's your sense of adventure?" she asked. Fearing for his sister, Oliver tried to sway her from her risky plan. "Lilly, you'll be in big trouble if Heidi finds out what you're gonna do." he said, shaking his head. He was sure, their person would die a thousand deaths, if any of her pets went missing. "Well, I guess I'll just hope she doesn't catch wind of this." Lilly said. "And besides, my ride to school would be an educational experience we'd all benefit from. So, I'm pretty sure, Heidi will be okay with it." Lilly reasoned. Meanwhile, Clyde knew better than to believe her. "Lilly, are you out of your mind? Do you honestly believe, Heidi will be okay with you hitching a ride on a school-bus, and touring across town without her?" he asked. "And besides, I don't see, how your ride to school, could benefit any of us." he said, giving her a look. "Seriously, Clyde, you need to chill-out. I'm sure, she won't mind. And besides, I promise to tell you all about my day, just as soon as I get home." she said, hoping to put his mind at ease. "Nice try, Lilly, but I'm still not buying it." he said, shaking his head. "Then just come with me, Clyde." "I don't want to." "Oh, come on. Don't be such a chicken." "Lilly, neither of us thinks it's a good idea." Pierre said, coming to his brother's defense. "I understand, and I appreciate your concern, Poodle, but trust me, I know what I'm doing." she said, turning to Oliver. "You'll come with me, won't you, Ollie?" "Sorry, Lilly, but I think I'll pass." he said. "Fine, be that way, but I bet old, Tino here, will come with me, won't you, little buddy." she said, patting him on the back. But sure enough, he declined the opportunity too. So, with that, Lilly knew she was outnumbered. "Suit yourselves, you guys, but you'll be missing out, on a golden opportunity to explore the unexplored." she said, trying one last time to entice them. But alas, she was on her own. Eager for adventure, Lilly knew that come first thing in the morning, she'd carry out her daring plan to ride the bus to school.

2 *A New Adventure Awaits*

AS THE MORNING COMMUTE PROGRESSED, so did the ever-present sound of motorists driving past the house. The early part of June gave way to azaleas and rhododendrons in rich full bloom, offering splashes of color to the modest front yard. Bumble bees danced from flower to flower, collecting their nectar and pollen, while the black-capped chickadees perched high upon the maple trees sang their song.

Streams of sunshine filtering through the window blinds, served as nature's alarm clock. As the sun began to rise, so did the sleepy household. The coffeepot came to life, announcing a new day, filling the house with a rich aroma. With a stretch and a yawn, Heidi pulled back the sheets, and padded her way to the kitchen, where she was greeted by her trio of cats, Buddy, Buster, and Sassy. The three purring felines, gathered at her feet, eagerly awaited their morning meal, as she generously filled their bowl with fish flavored kibble. Buddy was first to begin the crunching fest, savoring every crumb. His coat of blue-tinted gray, stood out against that of Buster's gray, and white stripes. The two hungry cats, sat hunched over their bowl, devouring every morsel. Conversely, Sassy's show of disinterest was purposeful in the way she sauntered to the food dish, displaying little interest in her human's kind offering. As a self-proclaimed diva, Sassy's fluffy coat of black, and white, with splashes of gold, lent her the look of elegance. She was considered bold and bodacious, and oftentimes, intolerant of her easy-going brothers.

Finally, basking in the morning glow, the cats sat perched in the window, licking their paws, and digesting their meal. Meanwhile, the dogs began their morning routine of nosing around the backyard. There, they eagerly, dug their holes, and kicked up dirt, delighting in the scents, the night left behind. Then remembering her plan, Lilly made her way to the gate. Harnessed in her wheel-cart, she was ready to go. Noticing the kids, gathered across the street, she knew the bus was well, on its way. And so, she assumed, with one swift push, the gate would swing wide open, thus freeing her from the yard. But alas, she quickly realized, the gate was locked, and her sneaky plan came crashing to a screeching halt. "Oh no! Now what am I going to do?" she asked, looking hopelessly up at the latch. "It's okay, Lilly. I'm sure one of us will think of something." Clyde said, hoping to pacify his venturous sister. "But, Clyde, nobody here is tall enough to reach the lock." Puffing out his chest, Clyde was determined to save the day. "Never fear, super Clyde is here!" he said, jumping at the gate, determined to unlock it. But after a few failed attempts, the pudgy shih tzu looked hopelessly at the lock that seemed miles out of anyone's reach.

Refusing to give up, Lilly looked to Pierre, and suggested the unthinkable... "Poodle, do me a favor will ya, sweetie? Just let Clyde here, stand on your shoulders so he can reach the lock for me." she said, keeping her voice sugary sweet. Stunned by her request, Pierre knew he didn't have the strength to carry the weight of his overly nourished brother. "Um, Lilly, no offense to Clyde, but my old bones can barely hold my own weight, let alone chubster's." he said, referring to his brother. With that, Clyde took offense. "Excuse me, Pierre, but are you implying that I might have a weight problem?" Pierre shook his head. "No, not at all, Clyde. If you ask me, yours is more of a snacking problem." With that, Clyde's level of defense ratcheted. "Oh, is that so, Pierre? Well, for your information, I don't have a so-called, *snacking problem.* I prefer to call it, *palate pampering.* And besides, I don't think a few pizza scraps here and there ever hurt anyone." he said, in his own defense.

Meanwhile, Lilly had no tolerance for her brother's argument, as she knew, time was of the essence. "Will you guys knock it off? Did you forget I have a bus to catch?" she asked, turning her attention to Oliver. "Will you give it a try, Ollie? I bet you could reach the lock... After all, you are pretty tall." she said, hoping he'd oblige. Oliver shook his head. "No way,

Lilly. I don't want to be the one responsible for letting you out of the yard." he said. "Oh, come on... Please, Ollie. I'll take full blame for everything. I promise." And with that, Oliver relented, even though it was against his better judgment. Standing tall on the tips of his paws, the lanky dog stretched as high as he could, but alas, the gate latch was out of his reach too. "Well, Lilly. You're out of luck. Looks like you're not going anywhere." Oliver said. But Lilly wasn't one to give up that easily. "Not so fast, Ollie. I still have one more trick up my sleeve." she said, turning her attention to the oldest and smallest of brothers. "Tino, how would you like to be the hero of the day?" she asked, in her sweetest voice. With that, the decrepit poodle slowly turned his face to hers. His cloudy eyes revealed his senior years, as the cataracts obscuring his vision matched his downy white coat. With her face close to the wise, hearing-impaired poodle, Lilly spoke in a raised tone. "TINO, I NEED YOU TO CLIMB UPON OLIVER'S BACK AND UNLOCK THE GATE. WILL YOU DO THAT FOR ME?" With a slight nod of his head, the pint-size dog obliged, and slowly worked his way towards Oliver. Finally, sitting awkwardly atop his brother's shoulders, an unsteady posture suggested an imminent fall. Recognizing the dangers, Clyde advised against what his sister was asking the old dog to do. "I don't think this is such a good idea, Lilly." he said, shaking his head. "Be quiet, Clyde. You'll ruin his concentration." Lilly snapped. After that, nobody dared speak a word. They watched with bated breath, as Tino continued his courageous balancing act.

Breaking the silence, Buster called from the second-floor window. "Lilly, you're gonna be in big trouble if Heidi finds out what you're doing." Giving him a look, Lilly didn't feel the need to qualify her actions. "Well, Buster, she'll never know unless you tell her. So, please do me a favor, and just mind your own business." she said, keeping her eye on Tino. Just then, Sassy noticed the bus making the turn. "You'll never make it!" she warned. Despite the pressure, Lilly refused to give up, and continued to encourage Tino to stay on task. "C'mon little guy. You can do this. I just know you can." she said, watching him steady himself, as she knew, one wrong move, and he'd come toppling down. But the old dog was determined. Reaching for the lock, he teetered on the tips of his paws, working to keep his balance. Suddenly, he began to wobble. All who watched were sure that Tino was about to fall, but miraculously, the little dog regained his footing, and everyone could breathe a sigh of relief. Revered for his fearlessness, Tino's slight frame stood in stark contrast to his enormous bravery, as he continued his courageous efforts. "You can do it, Tino." Lilly encouraged, keeping her voice low. Meanwhile, Oliver was doing his best to remain perfectly still, but a tingle in his nose signaled an impending sneeze. He fought against the urge, but alas, the explosive sneeze shot like a canon, straight from his mouth. All watched in horror, as Tino launched like a rocket, high into the air. But with his quick thinking, the wise, old dog, disengaged the latch, causing the gate to swing wide open. Finally, landing with a soft thump, Tino sat dazed and confused, while Lilly ran celebratory circles around him. "Yay! Tino, you did it! You really did it! You're my hero!" she shouted, applauding his success. Realizing her opportunity, Lilly sped past the opened gate, wheelchair in all, and headed straight towards the bus-stop. "Adios, amigos! I'll see you after school!" she hollered, as she raced out of sight...

3 *The Connection*

T HE WALKWAY SEEMED AN ENDLESS path. With her wheels in tow, Lilly darted across the street towards the modest congregation. Pulling herself harder and faster, burning breathes caught in her throat as adrenaline coursed her veins. Finally, joining the kids with only moments to spare, she was welcomed with adoring smiles and gentle pats to her head. Surrounded by boundless attention, Lilly looked up to see one girl who stood back from the group. Absent from her face was a smile that could have easily added to her innocent beauty. Her tresses black as night, fell gently past her narrow shoulders and down her slender back. Springy ringlets delicately framed her youthful face, casting her in an angelic light. The morning sunshine bathed her flawless skin, adding to her look of softness. Her eyes, deep pools of dark brown, pulled with a penetrating stare. The girl and the dog remained locked in a gaze, until the bus pulled to the stop, thus barging in, on their wordless conversation.

The bright yellow motor-coach stood before them rumbling with life; long bifold doors pulled open wide, revealed the driver sitting tall behind the wheel. His jolly voice was easily heard over the noisy engine as he greeted his students. "Good morning boys and girls." he said. His laughing eyes became mere slits, as a wide smile spread across his time-worn face. Rays of sun, streamed through fine wisps of hair atop his head, casting him in a soft glow that matched his gentle smile. Welcomed by their driver, the children climbed aboard the bus, adorning their backpacks, and sneakers, and plopped into the long row of seats. Meanwhile, Lilly remained harnessed in her wheel-cart, hopelessly watching, as each student ascended the tall stairs, and disappeared inside the bus. Conquering the mountainous stair-climb seemed an impossible feat, she thought. Fearing her ride would leave without her, she contemplated her next move. Just then, the lonely-eyed girl stopped short, noticing Lilly, in her wheels. Daring ideas swirled in her mind, as she prepared to execute her bold act.

Noticing the bus driver's distraction, the young girl, saw her opportunity, and acted fast. Her lips curved upward in a mischievous way, as she contemplated her next move. Prepared to do the unthinkable, her cheeks dimpled, as a sneaky smile spread across her face. After exchanging a knowing look, the girl and dog, prepared for what would happen next... In an instant, the girl reached for Lilly, and swiftly pulled her up the steps, before ushering her down the long row of seats. The aisle seemed an endless run, as they quickly worked their way to the back. Finally, with the little dog, ducked below the seat, the girl worked to catch her breath. Adrenaline coursed her veins, causing her legs to tremble, as her actions left her feeling, light years beyond her comfort zone. In time, her breaths began to slow, and she took pleasure in knowing, the little dog was close by. They shared their ride to school, but it would be their emotional journey, neither would soon forget...

As the bus moved along, the girl stared out the window. Her unblinking gaze suggested she was miles away, in deep thought. The ripple effect of her bold move would surely alter her day, she thought. And perhaps her life would change too, as a foreign sense of empowerment, washed over her. Meanwhile, Lilly remained hidden below the seat, looking up, at her daydreaming friend, and wondered, what thoughts she might be churning. Sensing the dog's stare, the girl broke from her trance, instantly noticing the charm adorning Lilly's neck. Curiously, she began to inspect the engraved piece, that bore a name on one side, and a finely etched lily, on the other. Intrigued by the dog's neck attire, the girl further scrutinized the intricate charm. Her dark brown eyes, narrowed below her delicate brow, as she whispered aloud the inscription... "Princess Lilly." she said. "Your name is, Lilly?" she asked, keeping to a whisper. "It's nice to make your acquaintance." Delighted to have made a new friend, the young girl's eyes widened, as her lips curved into a gentle smile, revealing an inner joy. Lilly looked to the girl with an adoring gaze, and listened intently as she once again, began to speak... "My name is, Jade." she softly, whispered. The sound of her voice sparked a reactionary bark, catching Jade by surprise. "Shhh... quiet down, Lilly. The others will hear you." she said, looking around, ensuring the safety of her secret. And so, it was then, the two sat and silence, sharing a mutual trust in spite of the newness of their friendship, never anticipating the adventurous journey that lay ahead...

4 *Monkey See Monkey Do*

S TANDING DUMFOUNDED AT THE OPENED gate, the other dogs watched as Lilly sped out of sight. Her brazen act had a contagious effect, and it wasn't long before her sudden departure sparked a combined sense of adventure for the ones she left at home. Before long, they too, were planning an excursion of their own… "Well, we can't just sit here, and hope that Heidi doesn't notice Lilly missing. We have to do something." Clyde said, looking to the others. "So, what are you suggesting, Clyde?" Oliver dared to ask. "Well, I think it's our duty to do, what any good brother would." he said, but his vague answer, yielded more questions… "Clyde, stop speaking in riddles, and just tell us what you're trying to say?" Oliver said, feeling annoyed. "Okay, fine. I was thinking, maybe Lilly was right when she told me I should take chances and broaden my horizons. So, why not? Let's just go look for her." Shaking his head, Oliver was quick to disagree. "Are you out of your mind, Clyde?" "Listen Ollie, somebody's gotta bring her home." he said. "I know, but I'm pretty sure, the four of us drudging across town, isn't the answer. And besides, we don't even know where the bus took her." Oliver reasoned. "Oh, c'mon Ollie, let's just do it. I mean, how hard could it be to track her scent? Less we forget, a dog's nose, knows." Feeling the pressure, Oliver eventually agreed. Clyde then looked to Pierre. "So, Poodle, you're coming too, right?" Pierre was quick to answer. "Absolutely! It'd be a shame to waste this opened gate, opportunity." he said, rearing to go. Clyde nodded. "Good. I'm glad you see it my way, Pierre. Now, let's see at how Tino feels about it." Clyde said, looking to his eldest brother. "TINO, DO YOU AGREE THAT WE SHOULD GO LOOKING FOR LILLY?" he asked, in a raised tone. Sure enough, old Tino slowly turned, and gave a nod of approval... So, it was then, the search for Lilly commenced... Oliver took the lead, carrying Tino on his back, while Pierre and Clyde followed closely behind them. The four of them worked their way down the busy roadway, eager for adventure, but oblivious to the prevailing dangers, they'd soon encounter...

5 Leap of Faith

A long parade of buses pulled up to the school. Rows of bright yellow, filled the space as far as the eye could see, while bus after bus, rolled to a stop in front of the three-story building. Their tall, bi-fold doors pulled open wide, released a flood of students, as the school-bell rang out loud, and announced the start of class. Meanwhile, Jade sat at the back of the bus, with Lilly ducked by her feet. She soon realized her predicament, as she hopelessly watched each student before her, abandoned their seat, and make their way to the front. As the bus began to empty, so did Jade's hopes of keeping her stowaway a secret. Then, just as she feared, the boy seated before her, turned and spotted Lilly, hiding by her feet. He raised his brow in shock, stunned to see the dog who wore wheels, riding the school bus. Jade was sure he was about to alert the driver. Then, as if on que, the bus-driver called from the front to the students lingering at the back. "Hurry along now, boys and girls, or you'll be late for class." he said. With that, the boy turned as if contemplating what to do next. His cheek dimpled, as a sneaky smile spread across his face. Jade's heart sank as she looked to him with beseeching eyes. "Cody, please don't tell." she implored. Her whispering voice was a mere quiver of desperation. Despite her pleas, Cody made his way down the aisle towards the driver. His slight frame balanced his oversized backpack that bore pterodactyls and dinosaurs. Finally, making his way to the front, he stopped short by the bus-driver's side.

Jade was sure at that moment, Cody would reveal her secret. She remained at the back, begging him wordlessly with her penetrating stare, until resigning to the inevitable. She should have known better than to believe she'd get away with sneaking a dog on the bus in the first place, she thought. And so, she waited for the ax to fall... But alas, what happened next, was not at all what she expected. Without warning, Cody purposely threw himself down the steps of the idling bus, and began his phony cries of pain. Shocked by what she saw, Jade jumped from her seat, believing that her classmate was seriously hurt. Meanwhile, the driver sprang into action, and began to aid his seemingly injured student. Cody's exaggerated cries could be heard from across the school-grounds, catching the attention of all the other students. He implemented his best acting skills, working to distract the group, gripping his ankle, and pretending to be an agonizing pain.

Students from all around, swarmed the area, curious about their injured classmate. Realizing Cody's perfectly, thought-out diversion, Jade saw her opportunity. So, acting fast, she pulled on her backpack, and pushed open the emergency door at the rear of the bus. Then, leaping from the four-foot drop, she turned to Lilly, who stood harnessed in her wheel-cart. Jade knew, there was no way, the little dog could safely jump from such a height. Meanwhile, Lilly looked ahead with the looming drop before her, as Jade did her best to coax her along. "Lilly, don't be afraid. Jump, and I'll catch you." she promised. At that moment, Jade's confidence was strong, but Lilly wondered if the young girl had the physical strength to match. With time running short, she knew she had to make her move. With her paws pressed against the floor of the bus, she looked once again, beyond the opened door. One more step was all it would take before falling to the ground, she thought. Meanwhile, Jade remained with her arms outstretched, determined to catch her. "Lilly, I promise, I won't let you fall." she said. Meanwhile, Cody continued his ruse, determined to keep the others distracted. Lilly knew, it was now or never, as she worked up the courage to take the leap of faith. The forbidding drop loomed before her, while Jade stood ready, and waiting. Her backpack hung from her narrow shoulders, as her petite frame strained under the weight of her load. "Lilly, jump now!" she urged, as she knew, Cody wouldn't be able to distract the others for much longer. It was then, Lilly put her trust in the girl who promised to catch her. So, with her eyes squeezed closed, she launched herself from the platform, causing the wheels of her cart to spin wildly behind her. Meanwhile, Jade stood ready with her arms opened wide, prepared to catch the flying dog. Like slow-motion, Lilly moved through the air, until finally, landing safely into Jade's waiting arms. Without a moment to spare, the girl and the dog took off, running... Finally, taking cover behind a dumpster, they remained hidden, and silently, celebrated their triumphant feat. Sitting huddled, they worked to catch their breath, but little did they know, their victorious moment would be short-lived, and things were about to go horribly wrong...

6 Searching for Lilly

T AKING ADVANTAGE OF THE OPENED gate, the dogs began their adventurous search for their sister. Moving throughout the city, there was no doubt that the four of them would find themselves in a few precarious situations, for it was their lack of street smarts that would ultimately hinder their success. Picking up on Lilly's scent would be easy enough, especially if Tino's nose lead the group. But in the end, it would be their combined sense of curiosity that would easily lead them astray. Oliver did his best to keep everyone on task, but it was Clyde's insatiable appetite that would oftentimes cloud his thinking and Pierre's innate desire to chase anything that moved, is what would easily steer them off course...

The sleeping city came to life with commuters, delivery trucks and school buses, all whizzing past. The fast-moving traffic came dangerously close to the adventure seeking dogs. Oliver took the lead, carrying Tino atop his back, while

Pierre and Clyde followed closely behind, all doing their best to hug the side of the road. Their hanging tongues suggested an increased thirst, but they'd soon find out, a parched palate would be the least of their worries...

Riding high, upon Oliver's back, Tino kept his keen nose in the air, as he worked to pick up, on Lilly's scent. Clyde wasn't far behind, working his short legs, doing his best to keep up with Oliver's long strides. Pierre was last in line with his nose to the ground, absorbing every floral, and earthy scent his nose could detect. The four of them continued their trek down Main Street, in search of their sister, motivated by the love and concern they had for her. Bound by circumstance, they moved along, indulging in private thoughts, as they recalled their days of homelessness... *The city pound was far from a place of joy and contentment. It was a place, where pungent fumes of urine and feces, combined with the burning odor of disinfectant, dug at their nasal membranes. Locked in a kennel, there was no way to escape their waking nightmare. Plagued with fear and boredom, they'd oftentimes, will themselves to fall asleep; a futile attempt to escape the monotony of their lonely existence. Mournful cries from other abandoned dogs, echoed off the tall ceilings, created an unbearable cacophony; sounds of which will never be forgotten.* Over time, they were able to put behind a life of loneliness, as their love, and commitment to each other, flourished in their newly adoptive home. And so, it was then, their search for Lilly continued, and the four of them courageously, made their way across town...

7 A Close Call

JADE'S POUNDING HEART, FELT IT would burst through her chest, as a searing burn, clawed at her throat, causing her to wince with every breath she took. Her legs trembled beneath her, as adrenaline coursed her veins like a raging river. Standing hunched with her hands on her knees, she slowly recovered from her sprint across the schoolyard. Meanwhile, Lilly remained by her side, harnessed in her wheelie. Her draping tongue revealed her pure exhaustion, as she too, felt the effects of their mad-dash from the bus. Hidden behind the dumpster, Jade marveled at her success in sneaking Lilly from the bus. An amazing feat it was, she thought. But so much was running through her mind at that moment, as she found herself surrounded by bags full of trash. Surely, nobody would find them hidden amidst the garbage, she thought. Meanwhile, Lilly stood close by, curious about her new surroundings. She lifted her nose to the pungent odor of sour milk permeating throughout the space, while her pricked ears, turned to the soft hum emitting from the building's cooling system. Then looking to Jade, she could tell she was miles away, lost in deep thought. Determined to get her attention, she offered soft licks to the daydreaming girl's chin, thus, pulling her back from her silent journey. A slow emergence from a self-defined comfort zone, was taking place, as Jade began to find the emotional strength to shatter the chains of self-doubt. For it was because of Lilly's boundless bravery, she felt inspired in a way she never thought possible. Wrought with emotion, tears streamed down her face.

Lilly remained close, wordlessly comforting the crying girl with the mere essence of her presence. Jade welcomed the dog's comforting ways, as oftentimes, she was the target of the school's ruthless personality, and bullying became a constant source of extreme distress. Rilee was well-known for her merciless attacks. She'd unleash on those she set her sights, seeming to take pleasure in causing others emotional pain. Over time, her unremorseful actions took a toll, causing Jade duress for months on end. Filled with emotion, she looked to Lilly with lashes wet with tears, before giving way to painful sobs... "I love you, Princess Lilly." she whispered. Lilly's heart crumbled at the sight of Jade's tears, and so, she began to lick the drops from the crying girl's quivering chin. With that action, Jade giggled despite her sadness, and smiled through glistening eyes, as it was the dog, who brought her the long-awaited joy she so desperately craved. "Lilly, promise you'll never leave me." she said.

Pulling herself close, Lilly bathed in the warmth of the young girl's soft breath. And so, it was then, Jade knew she had a friend for life. A smile spread across her face, washing away her look of sadness. Then suddenly, their moment of joy was harshly interrupted... A strong and familiar voice called out from the front of the dumpster. "May I ask, what you are doing back there, young lady?" Instantly startled, Lilly backed herself further into the corner, in an effort to remain hidden, just as Jade jumped at the sound of the authoritative voice. "I'm sorry, Mister Alan. I was just..." she started to say, but he cut her off mid-sentence. "I don't want your apologies, or your excuses, Jade. Hurry along now, and get to class." he said, sharply. In an instant, Jade was on her feet. Her slight frame carried an enormous heart, and her bravery was quickly growing to match. Brushing herself off, she turned to Lilly who remained ducked in the corner. Their eyes met, sharing a mutual concern. Fearing it was their last moments together, Jade maintained her gaze, before slowly, turning to leave. Lilly remained in her hiding spot, fighting the urge to follow, and sadly watched as Jade walked away... Nobody dared to challenge Mister Alan. As the principal of the school, he was always neatly dressed, which matched his need for order. So, to discover one of his students where she shouldn't have been, conflicted with his obsessive quest for all things be just so.

It was then, Mister Alan began to sense that Jade was hiding something. His curiosity piqued, as he was drawn to the corner in which Lilly was hiding. Hit with a wave of panic, Jade watched as he slowly made his way to the back of the dumpster. With no place to retreat, Lilly backed herself, further into the tight spot, doing her best to remain hidden. There, she stood uncomfortably still, for she knew, even the slightest of sounds, would easily lead to her discovery. Then, without warning, a squeak from her wheel-cart caught his ear. Lilly's eyes grew wide with paralyzing fear, as she was sure he'd soon find her hiding in the corner. Jade could see that things were getting too close for comfort. So, with her quick thinking, she pretended to cough uncontrollably, thus drawing Mister Alan's attention away from Lilly's hiding spot. Just as she hoped, he grew concerned by her sudden illness, and began to escort her to the health office. Although it tore at her heart to leave Lilly behind, Jade thought to do otherwise, would impose consequences she wasn't willing to face. So, without much choice, she continued her ruse, while her make-believe coughs were heard as she walked out of sight...

8 *Pep Talk*

A ROW OF EMPTY CHAIRS lined the far wall of the health office. There, Jade remained slumped in her chair with her overly-filled backpack, plopped on her lap. Her thoughts trailed back to Lilly, while she sat there, waiting for the school nurse. She was still reeling from the close call with Mister Alan, but thanks to her quick thinking, her make-believe cough did the trick, and he never noticed Lilly, hiding behind the dumpster. But Jade knew it wouldn't be long before the nurse eventually figured out that she was never really sick to begin with. So, without much choice, all she could do, was wait to be seen. She was eager to get back to Lilly, and was concerned about leaving her alone. Assuming she was scared, Jade worried all the more, which further added to the agonizing passage of time. Sitting there, attempts to distract herself proved futile, as she watched the nurse's secretary, conduct her office duties. The delicate ringing of multiple phone lines caught her ear, while the faint odor of newly installed carpet, tapped at her nose. In the end, her distraction was brief, and it was all she could do, to sit there, and patiently wait. Feeling down on herself, Jade failed to see her full potential in all things, despite her talent for singing. And although her melodic voice was adored by many, she lacked the ability to recognize an inner magic, kept deep within her soul.

At times, Jade felt safest, keeping silent, and hiding behind emotional walls that protected her from rejection. But since meeting Lilly, she began to emerge from her hideaway, and no longer would she allow the monster she called, "fear" grip her soul and chase away her dreams. Oftentimes, losing herself in a peaceful world that only her imagination could provide, Jade was free to allow her sleeping spirit to awaken. With a creative power, she envisioned herself on a stage in front of a cheering crowd... *The audience adored her. Applauding and tossing flowers, the crowd begged for more. There, she stood captivating the group, waving with a smile that lit up the platform and a voice that carried you away... Her devoted audience chanted wanting to hear more of her perfect voice. "Encore! Encore!"* ... Suddenly, the office door pushed open, waking her from her happy daydream. Caught by surprise, Jade looked up to see a young man emerge. He greeted her with an extended hand and a welcoming smile. Although he wasn't a male model, he could have passed for one, with his sun-kissed hair, stylishly parted to one side, and neatly trimmed above his ears, framing his perfect face. With eyes of vivid blue, and flecks of green, he wore a genuine smile that lit up his face, as the curve of his lip revealed perfectly aligned teeth. His Gap-style clothes lent him a youthful look, as he padded across the carpeted floor. "Good morning, Jade." he said. "The kids call me, J.C. Let's go take a seat in my office." he said, motioning for her to follow. Standing at the threshold, her eyes were drawn to the sports memorabilia covering the walls of the small windowless space. Displayed on the edge of his desk, a framed photo of a young girl and toddler boy caught her eye. "Those are my children." he explained. Jade stood staring at the photograph. The little girl staring back was the epitome of happiness with her laughing eyes. "We named her Marlee Hope, and my son, Charlie Carter." he said, beaming with pride. Taking a seat, J.C. motioned for Jade to do the same. She lifted herself onto the chair in front of his desk, leaving her backpack on the floor. She was expecting to meet with the nurse, not the guidance counselor. He seemed nice enough, she thought, and took comfort in knowing he had children of his own. Sitting there, she silently, questioned the reason for their meeting, as she nervously, looked around his office, until finally, noticing the nameplate at the front of his desk that read, "Jeremy Craig." Dawning on her, "J.C." was short for the guidance counselor's name. "Would you prefer to call me, Jeremy?" he asked, seeming to have read her mind. Jade nodded, as a slight smile spread across her face. "Then it's settled. You can call me, Jeremy." he said, returning the smile. Jeremy's role as guidance counselor suited him well.

Relating well with his students, his youthful appearance and carefree manner, always put his students at ease, hence why they addressed him by his first name. "Jade, I know you were sent to the office to see the nurse, but quite frankly, I don't think your "cough" is the concern. Look around this office and tell me what you see." he said, motioning with his hand. Doing as he asked, she took in the images covering the walls. Framed photographs of well-known sport's heroes decorated the space, all symbolizing one thing, to believe in yourself. Jeremy could see a lacking in his student's confidence, and it concerned him that she didn't recognize her own incredible potential. He stood leaning against the front of his desk. There before him, Jade remained seated with her eyes on her lap. "Jade, I've been thinking, you should consider entering this year's talent contest." She looked up in surprise, for he suggested the unthinkable. "I don't think I could." she said. Her meek voice matched the weakness of her confidence. Averting her eyes, she listened once more, as Jeremy preached her self- worth. "Jade, listen to me. You can do anything you set your mind to. Just as the people in these photographs believed in themselves, you should too." he said, motioning around the room. The two remained quiet, as she digested his words. An awkward silence filled the office, for even a pin-drop would sound as a thunderous boom. Suddenly, catching them both by surprise, a panicked call for help, sounded from the overhead paging system...

"ATTENTION! Help is needed in the gymnasium! A dog wearing a set of wheels is running wildly around the court!" shrieked the voice. Jeremy immediately shot to the door. "Jade, I'll be right back. I've got to go see what's going on in Mister B's gym class." he said, dashing from the office. *Saved by the bell*, Jade thought, as she was more than ready to end the meeting with the guidance counselor. Assuming the dog wearing wheels was Lilly, she figured the little dog must have found a way into the school. A smile spread across her face, as she began to entertain the comical possibilities. If Lilly made the scene, there was no doubt that Mister B's gym class would have taken on a whole new level of excitement, and she wasn't about to miss one minute of the action. So, with that notion, Jade too, bolted from the office and hurried her way to the gym...

9 Chaos on the Main

MAKING THEIR WAY DOWN MAIN street, Tino could be seen sitting high upon Oliver's back with his nose in the air. His superior sense of smell was second to none, despite his senior years. Clyde and Pierre followed closely behind, also employing their sniffing skills. But as usual, Clyde was drawn to the occasional scent of food wafting past. "I'm calling a break. Any one up for a donut?" he hollered from the back of the line. Oliver shook his head. "Clyde, we're not on a quest for sugar-filled pastries, so you can satisfy your snacking urges. We're supposed to be out here looking for Lilly." he said, giving his brother a look. So, without another word, the ever-hungry shih tzu, continued his trek, but when it came to his appetite, Clyde wouldn't give up that easily...

As the morning progressed, so did the city's road construction. The dogs eventually found themselves caught up in the midst of a congested work-zone. With every step they took, they carefully worked to navigate their way around ditches and work trucks. The percussive blare from a jackhammer pounded at their eardrums, while impenetrable road-dust filled their nostrils and clouded their vision. Just up ahead, a monstrous backhoe clawed at the crumbling tar, creating deep holes in the roadway, threatening to swallow anyone who dared pass. Further down the road, an elephant sized cement-mixer truck, rumbled at an idle. Liquid concrete, poured like lava from its turning drum, sure to stop anyone in their tracks. All throughout the work area, orange cones marked driving lanes for motorist, slowly working their way past, as heavy loads of liquid cement were skillfully, smoothed into, soon-to-be sidewalks.

A slow row of cars made their way past the busy construction zone. Shimmers of heat, rose from a long line of scorching metal rooftops, while impatient motorists leaned on their car horns, determined to get to who knows where. Standing amidst the chaos, Corey waved drivers past, ensuring their safety, while roadwork ensued all around him. It was just an average day on the job for the young police officer. Tall and lean, Corey was the epitome of handsome. His distinct cheekbones and angular jaw lent him a look of authority. The brim of the cap, pulled low over his eyes, added to his commanding looks. Surrounded by traffic, he anticipated a long day on his feet, but despite the added ten pounds his duty belt offered, his strength and stamina, would go unmatched. All seemed an ordinary day, as far as road details were concerned. But little did Corey know, four nervous dogs were heading his way, and his day was about to become anything, but ordinary.

Up and down the roadway, the crew busily conducted their laborious work. As far as the eye could see, hard hats and bright orange work-vests, were the common theme. A low and steady rumble from massive work trucks, could be heard throughout the work area, while plumes of road-dust, added to the clustered space. It was then, a worker spotted something heading his way. Mirage-like images, rising from the burning pavement, moved in his direction, before he realized, four thirsty dogs were making their way down the graveled road. Resting his gloved hand on the end of his shovel, he focused his gaze once more. The whites of his eyes stood out, against the black road-dust, marring his face. Curious by the unexpected visitors, he alerted the police officer who stood close by. "Corey, it looks like we have company coming." he said, with a chuckle. Turning, Corey first spotted Tino, sitting tall upon Oliver's back. The two of them worked their way down the dangerous path, narrowly missing deep trenches along the way. Clyde and Pierre came next, clumsily, navigating their way past the dust-filled zone. Realizing the dog's dangerous predicament, Corey held up his hand, determined to stop the flow of traffic. Eager to alert the drivers, he blew hard into his whistle, but the shrill was swallowed by the pre-existing noise. Acting fast, he lifted his sunglasses, and focused his gaze once more. His blue-green eyes, reminiscent of a stormy sea, could easily drown you in his intense look. His features, like chiseled granite, were strong and defined, added to his stern look of authority. He stood calculating his next move, and grew increasingly concerned, as motorists drove dangerously close to the seemingly lost dogs. Determined to get the drivers attention, he blew once more into his whistle, but the ear-piercing shrill, caught Oliver's ear, causing him to startle. The panicked dog, frantically bolted down the dust-filled area, bumping into cones, while Tino held on like a cowboy, riding a bucking bronco. Clyde and Pierre fared no better, as they ran spooked in front of a trail of moving cars, forcing drivers to stop short, and lean on their horns, which added to the clamor and confusion. The blaring noise pounded merciless at the dog's ears. Realizing he needed help, Corey called for Champ, his loyal, canine partner. Rescued from a litter of pups, Champion trained well as the perfect, police-dog. In time, he and Corey became the ultimate, crime-fighting team. Nothing could get past Corey's vigilant eye, or Champ's superior sense of smell. Always at the ready, it took nothing more than a few short commands, before Champ sprang into action, and safely herded the dogs to the side of the road.

Finally, corralled alongside the police cruiser, the dogs settled themselves in a small slice of shade. Their thirsty tongues, hung low, after their hair-raising ordeal. Dodging cars, and avoiding deep trenches, was not what they'd bargained for, when they set out to find their sister. Realizing the dangers, they sat huddled, sharing the same look of fear, each secretly regretting their decision to leave the yard. They were a long way from the comforts of their own backyard, and neither of them were wise to travel in a bustling city. Champ looked sympathetically at the tired group, before he began his interrogation... "Are you boys out of your mind? Don't you know, a dog could get hurt, or worse out here with all this construction going on?" Oliver looked up at the oversized hound dog. "We were merely, looking for our sister, that's all. She bolted from the yard this morning." he said, looking exhausted. "Your sister is missing?" Champ asked. "Well, yes and no." Oliver said. Looking puzzled, Champ pressed for an answer. "Come on now, is she missing or not?" Oliver knew, when it came to Lilly, things weren't always easy to explain. So, he took a deep breath, and tried once again, to shed some light on their predicament. "You see, what happened was, Lilly hitched a ride on a school bus this morning. We figure, she's on her way to school, but we're not really sure. We were hoping to track her down and bring her home before our human noticed any of us missing from the yard." "Oh, I see now." Champ said, nodding his head. Everything was beginning to make sense. He knew then, helping his fellow canines would be his priority. So, while his handler was busy dealing with the traffic-jam, Champ got acquainted with his new friends, and devised a plan to help them find their missing sister.

So, while Champ sat with the dogs, Corey directed the last of the cars past the work-zone. Meanwhile, curious drivers, stretched their necks to catch a glimpse of the roadside attraction. After all, a pack of seemingly, lost dogs, wandering throughout a busy traffic area, was not a common sight. Realizing the dangers, Oliver sat alongside the parked cruiser, with Tino clutched to his back. The last thing either of them wanted, was any more trouble. Conversely, Clyde and Pierre had other ideas in mind... Eager to satisfy an overpowering curiosity, each put their inquisitive nose to the ground, and pursued an exploration of the surrounding area. Before long, Clyde discovered an empty paper bag, once containing somebody's lunch. Even a few lingering food crumbs couldn't escape the ever-hungry shih tzu's appetite for a quick snack. Then plunging his face deep inside the sack, he began to scavenge for any food remnants his inquiring nose could detect. Suddenly, blinded by the bag, Clyde began a panicked run around the worksite. Running left and right, the frightened shih-tzu, frantically, worked to free himself from the dog-eating lunch-sack. Meanwhile, Pierre saw that his brother was in trouble, and ran to his aid, but in the process, the portly poodle, clumsily, tripped over a cone marker, and came dangerously close to falling into a vat of liquid cement. Watching the entire scene, Oliver shook his head at the mischievous duo, as drivers from both lanes, were forced to break hard, narrowly missing them. Luckily, Champ sprang into action, and leapt across the line of traffic, ultimately, preventing the clumsy pair from falling into a nearby drain-pipe ditch. Finally, the ever-vigilant police-dog managed to settle everyone alongside the police car once again, and ordered them to stay put. Meanwhile, Corey busily, worked to wave drivers past, in an attempt to clear the area. Suddenly, a radio call from inside the cruiser, caught his ear... *"Eight-eight-seven, to all available units. Attention, all available units. Back-up is needed at the Alan Taylor Middle School. A dog wearing wheels has been reported, running around the gymnasium. I repeat, a dog wearing wheels is running loose inside the gym."* Shaking his head, he couldn't believe his ears. His day was growing stranger by the minute. Then, reaching inside the cruiser, he responded to the call. "Unit four to eight-eight-seven... Unit four, is now in route to the Alan Taylor Middle School. *"Ten-four, unit four."* So, it was then, Corey prepared to head to the school, leaving the dogs with the road-crew.

Meanwhile, Champ overheard the radio call, and assumed the dog found at the school, was Lilly. So, when Corey's back was turned, the sly canine cop, began the sneaky task of ushering the dogs into the back of the cruiser. Oblivious to his stowaways, Corey jumped behind the wheel, and hit the gas. In an instant, the police car sped out of sight...

10 *School Daze*

J EREMY CONTINUED TO RACE DOWNSTAIRS. After hearing Mister Alan's panicked call for help, his first reaction was to assist with whatever crisis was ensuing in the gym. *A dog running wildly in the gym...* he thought, trying to envision such a sight. Taking the stairs two at a time, he finally turned the corner and bolted down the corridor leading to Mister B's gym class. In his youth, Jeremy excelled in competitive sports, and always did his best to keep in tip-top shape, but with a new baby in the house, a recent lack of sleep left him feeling depleted of any reserves. He figured, after his meeting with Jade, he'd stop by the cafeteria, and snag a mocha, iced coffee for a much-needed caffeine boost, but that would have to wait. Once arriving to the gym, he curiously, listened at the door... The echoing sounds of laughter, filtering through the walls, sounded more of a celebration than a crisis, he thought. Then pulling the door open, he took in the jaw-dropping sight, rousing him from his sleepy daze, faster than his favored iced-coffee ever could.

11 *Play Ball*

Earlier that morning…

E MERGING FROM HER HIDING SPOT, Lilly began an exploration of the grounds. The schoolyard devoid of any students, became eerily quiet with the start of class. Looking around, Lilly assumed that Jade must be somewhere, inside the school. Determined to find her, she worked the perimeter of the building, until discovering an open door, leading to the gym. The sounds of playful laughter, pouring from the doorway, caught her ear. But it was the elusive basketball, bounding up and down the court, that stole her attention. Tempted by its lure, she stood watching, as the fifth-grade gym-class was in full swing…

Brenden's whistle ripped through the air, echoing off the tall ceilings. "Foul!" he shouted. The acoustics allowed his

45

powerful voice to carry to the rafters. His structured teaching style matched his need for order. When met with opposition from any of his students, Brenden patiently reminded them of the rules of the game. On this day, it was Cody who challenged his gym teacher. "No way, Mister B. That wasn't a foul." "Nice try Cody, but this is a game of basketball, not a wrestling match." his gym-teacher said, with a wink.

Taking pride in his work, Brenden lead by example, believing that diligence and dedication were keys to success. With a nose to the grindstone mentality, he'd strive for perfection in all aspects, oftentimes, attacking things in a cerebral manor. Conversely, he also possessed a sense of humor that could draw even the moodiest of people, into a fit of laughter with his contagious chortle, and smiling, sky-blue eyes. Dressed for the job, his blue, cotton tee, clung to his perfectly carved muscles. Strong and statuesque, Brenden was the epitome of physical fitness. Complementing his shirt, his white shorts hung just above his knees, and a pair of high-top basketball shoes neatly completed his athletic ensemble. His honey-kissed hair clipped short with a hard part to one side, offered him a stylish flip. And while his striking looks could stop you in your tracks, it was the ear-piercing shriek of his whistle, that brought the entire gym-class to a halt. Standing tall with his clipboard in hand, Brenden paced the sidelines, carefully keeping score and instructing his students.

Cody stood amongst the other fifth graders on the court. The ankle injury from his "fall" earlier that morning seemed to have miraculously healed. And although his skill and speed were no match for some of the other kids, on this day, Cody seemed slightly off his game. His thoughts trailed back to the little, brown dog he found hiding on the bus earlier that morning. Remembering the way she looked up at him from below the seat tore at his heart, and he wondered what became of her after she took off running with Jade. Meanwhile, Brenden sensed his student's distraction and reminded him of the do's and don'ts of playing basketball. Standing on the free-throw line, Mister B quoted one of basketball's great Hall of Fame inductees. "The idea is not to block every shot. The idea is to make your opponent believe you might block every shot." And with that, he blew hard on the whistle and the game came back to life...

Meanwhile, Lilly remained in the doorway with a hawk's eye, fixed on the bouncing ball. Focusing her gaze, she watched as it danced across the wooden floor. Suddenly, losing all self-control, the adventurous, little dog, bolted onto the court with incredible speed, thus creating an uproar throughout the entire class. Surprised by their unexpected visitor, the children roared with laughter, as she continued her playful sprint around the gym. The happy sounds of giggling children echoed off the tall ceilings, and spilled out, into the hallways. Stunned by such a sight, Brenden began a futile attempt to restore order to his gym-class, but the screech of his whistle, fell on deaf ears. Caught up in the moment, Cody joined the lively run with the little, brown dog. His cheeks rose high upon his giggling face, pushing his eyes into mere slits. Playfully running together, they were the perfect picture of freedom and joy...

* * * *

Meanwhile, Jade wasn't far behind Jeremy, as she hastened down the stairs. A sense of relief brought a smile to her face, knowing Lilly was all right. But despite her solace, she never anticipated the little dog would have hijacked the fifth-grade gym-class. And with that final thought, Jade took the stairs, two at a time, and bolted down the corridor. This she had to see...

Once inside the gym, Jeremy spotted Brenden, standing on the sidelines, wearing a look of defeat. "Well, Mister B, it sure looks like your class is just a little out of control." His voice carried a silent laughter, but Brenden was fuming, and was in no mood for jokes. "No kidding, Jeremy. You think so?" he asked, in a voice drenched with sarcasm. "Hey, take it easy, Brenden. Why are you so edgy?" "Well, how do you expect me to feel? Fido, over there, wearing training wheels, just invaded my gym-class." "Oh c'mon, man. Lighten up, will ya? Brenden, where's the sense of humor we all know and love?" Jeremy asked, trying to lighten the mood. "Well, I'm sorry, but I don't think this is funny." "Listen, Brenden. A meeting with one of my students got interrupted because of the dog, so this doesn't affect just you." "Nice try Jeremy, but my whole class got turned upside down."

Paper In The Wind

* * * *

While chaos ensued in the gymnasium, Mister Alan waited outside for the police to arrive. He nervously, paced back and forth, and wondered how the wheelie-strutting dog, managed to get inside his school. The waiting seemed unbearable for the overly anxious principal, but to his relief, the approaching blue lights of Corey's cruiser, caught his worried eye. "Officer, please help me! There's a wild dog, running around my school!" "Calm down, Mister Alan, and show me where this wild dog of yours is." Corey said, shaking his head. He was sure the principal was overreacting. After all, nothing could compare to what he dealt with earlier that morning. *A wild dog*, he thought, smiling to himself. This he had to see...

Meanwhile, watching from the front seat of the cruiser, Champ kept a close eye on the two men as they disappeared inside the building. Assuming they wouldn't be gone long, the sneaky canine cop knew he'd have to act fast if he were to help the dogs he'd been hiding. "Okay everybody, let's move." he said, jumping from the car. One at a time, Clyde, Pierre, Oliver and Tino, eagerly leapt from backseat of the cruiser, and began to curiously nose around the school's parking lot. "So, now what?" Pierre asked, looking confused. "We look for Lilly, that's what." Champ said. "But, how, Champ? I mean, she could be anywhere by now." Shaking his head, Champ couldn't believe he had to explain the basic fundamentals of scent-tracking to a fellow canine. "Pierre, let me ask you a question. How long have you been a dog?" he asked. Puzzled by the question, Pierre gave his best answer. "All my life, I guess. Why do you ask?" Champ was doing his best to remain patient. "Pierre, take a good look at me. See this thing right here?" he asked, pointing to his face. "It's called, a nose. A dog sees more with his snout than he does with his eyes. C'mon now, this is dog-basics, 101. I'm surprised you don't already know this." Nodding, his head, Pierre was beginning to understand. After all, sniffing was his favorite pastime. Champ realized, Pierre was way out of his element, and understood the old dog's confusion. "Listen to me, Pierre. All I'm merely trying to tell you, is your nose will lead you to Lilly." It was then, everyone worked to pick up, on her scent. Tino maintained his seat atop Oliver's back, while the rest of the pack, busily tracked her around the building. It didn't take long before her familiar scent was detected alongside the dumpster. There, they were met with a variety of odors, both old and new. A pungent stink from yesterday's garbage lingered in, and around the oversized trash bin, instantly sparking Clyde's curiosity. A delectable array of food odors, wafted past his inquisitive nose, tempting the ever-hungry shih-tzu. Hoping to satisfy his rumbly tummy, Clyde volunteered to search the dumpster for their missing sister, an obvious ploy to indulge in a smelly snack. "Guys, I was thinking, maybe I should have a look inside. Who knows, Lilly might be trapped beneath a pile of trash-bags, and needs us to pull her out." he said, hoping for a dumpster diving opportunity. Wise to his brother's intent, Oliver firmly, objected. "Clyde, you and I both know, Lilly is not a damsel in distress, crying for help at the bottom of that pile of garbage. So, just admit it, you'd like nothing more than to submerge yourself and some kid's unfinished school-lunch, and fill your face like there was no tomorrow. It's a trash bin, Clyde, not an all-you-can-eat buffet." With that, the cunning shih-tzu looked up sheepishly, knowing his brother was right.

Looking ahead, Champ spotted an open door, leading to the gym. "Hey, guys, check this out." he said, keeping to a whisper. Doing their best to remain undetected, the other dogs tiptoed to the doorway, and peeked inside, instantly noticing Lilly on her wild run with the kids. "Look! There she is!" Pierre said excitedly, as he too, attempted to run onto the court. "Woah... not so fast, Poodle. We don't want anyone to know we're here." Champ said, stopping Pierre in his tracks. "But I don't understand, Champ. Why do we have to be so secretive?" Trying to remain patient, Champ went on to explain the importance of being subtle. "Pierre, listen to me. If the kids see a pack of dogs standing at the doorway, we're likely to create even more of a ruckus." Listening nearby, Clyde looked puzzled. "So, what are we supposed to do, just stand here and hope Lilly eventually sees us?" Champ shook his head. "Not exactly, Clyde. I have a surefire way of getting your sister's attention without the entire gym-class knowing we're here. You see, my handler keeps a whistle in his cruiser, audible only to a dog's ear. So, you see, once I can get ahold of that whistle, getting Lilly's attention will be a piece of cake." "Champ, you're a genius." Clyde said, patting him on the back. "And what did you say about, cake?"

* * * *

Meanwhile, standing at the opposite doorway, Corey took in the playful sight. It was plain to see, things had spiraled out of control in Brenden's class, but no emergency was taking place, he thought. Then, noticing the little dog wearing wheels, Corey jumped back when she sped past with a trail of giggling kids running after her. He smiled to himself, as he watched a perfect display of innocence and freedom, and thought it a shame that Mister Alan couldn't see the beauty of it all. But in the end, he knew it was his job to instill order. So, it was then, Corey began his attempts to reel the children from their playful frenzy.

Rubber soles squeaked against the wooden, gymnasium floor, as lively games of chase took place with the wheelie-strutting dog. Jeremy and Brenden worked to calm the rowdy group, but the kids were lost in a playful world, oblivious to anyone trying to get their attention.

"Hey, who called the cops?" Jeremy asked, noticing Corey, standing at the opposite side of the gym. "Beats me." Brenden said, shrugging his shoulders. "But I hope he does something about Fido over there." he said, referring to Lilly. Then, as if on que, Corey made his way across the busy court, dodging kids along the way. "Good morning, gentlemen. I'd say, this is more a situation for Animal Control, than it is the police." he said, referring to Lilly. "I couldn't agree more, officer." Brenden said. His frustration mounted as he explained the morning's events. "So, there I was, just minding my own business, instructing my students, when all of a sudden, a dog, pulling a chariot, shows up out of nowhere, and hijacks my gym-class." Standing close by, Jeremy couldn't contain his laughter, before Brenden shot him a look. "Oh, so you think this is funny?" "Yeah, I do actually. I mean, just look at the kids. They're having a ball." "Spoken like a true guidance counselor, Jeremy. You're always looking at things with an element of psychology." "Oh, come on, Brenden. Lighten up a little. All I meant was, it's not the end of the world because things shifted out of your sense of order. Remember, this affected my morning too." Brenden gave him a doubtful look. "I know, you already told me, your counseling session with one of your students got interrupted. But, that doesn't compare to what I'm dealing with." he said. Meanwhile, listening close by, Corey thought of his own encounter with dogs, earlier that morning. "So, you guys think you have it bad? Well, I'm pretty sure I got you both beat. Four dogs showed up, at my road-detail, this morning." Brenden looked up, in surprise. "Wait. What? Did you just say, *four* dogs?" he asked, wanting to know more. "So, what'd you do?" he asked. "There wasn't much I could do." Corey explained. "But thanks to my dog, Champ, we managed to corral them alongside my cruiser. The poor things got themselves jammed-up, pretty good." "So, where are they now?" Jeremy asked. "When headquarters dispatched the call,

I came here, and left them with the road-crew." Corey explained. "The poor things are probably lost." Brenden said, looking worried. But despite a mutual concern, Corey laughed to himself, as he recalled his morning's events. "What's so funny?" Jeremy asked, looking puzzled. "I'm remembering this one little dog I saw this morning. He was riding one of the other dogs like a prize show horse." Jeremy's face lit up. "No way! Are you serious?" he asked. Envisioning the sight, even Brenden, couldn't resist a smile, despite his frustration.

Suddenly, dawning on Corey, Champ, was still waiting in the cruiser. If anyone could corral the wheelie-strutting dog, it would be him, Corey thought. But little did he know, Champ was actually standing outside the gymnasium door with the other dogs, about to make their grand entrance, and the level of chaos was about to skyrocket out of control.

* * * *

Jade continued her mad dash to the gym. She was sick with worry, over Lilly's mischievous behavior, but was relieved to know, the little dog was safe, at least for the time being…Meanwhile, Brenden paced the sidelines, as his gym-class continued to blow out of control. He helplessly watched as his students continued their playful run, up and down the court, alongside the little, brown dog who wore wheels.

Champ stood at the open door, contemplating his next move. The idea of blowing the dog-whistle seemed logical enough, as it would enable to him to get Lilly's attention without alerting the entire gym-class class. The last thing he needed, was for everyone to notice a pack of dogs standing there at the door. He did his best to keep the other dogs calm, but when a dog's instinctive prey-drive kicked in, all bets were off. So, the five of them stood at the doorway, watching Lilly in an envious way, as she continued her playful run.

Finally, unable to resist the urge, Champ bolted onto the court like a galloping pony, joining in, on Lilly's chase of the runaway basketball. All heads turned, as the oversized hound, pranced around the gym, while his powerful barks, carried to the rafters, filling the space with his echoing yelps. Pierre entered next... Slipping on the polished, wooden floor, he did his best to keep up with Champ, but found himself sliding uncontrollably, across the court. Clyde next made the scene, making a beeline for the packed lunches left on the sidelines, as the ever-hungry shih-tzu never missed an opportunity for a snack. Finally, making their grand entrance, Oliver galloped onto the court with the speed of a racehorse, while Tino held on, riding him like a champion jockey. The comical duo created an uproar of laughter that poured from the gym.

Jade managed to get to the gym in time to witness the amusing sight. Watching from the doorway, the corners of her mouth, turned up in a slight smile, as a foreign sense of happiness tickled her soul. She gazed with unblinking eyes, as the dogs ran freely with the carefree group. Oh, how she longed to break from her emotional prison, and experience such a simple pleasure. For it was only in her daydreams, could she do so. Filled with peaceful thoughts, a sense of contentment hugged her spirit, as her imagination carried her to place where fear didn't exist. There, she lived without monsters who chased away her happiness. And so, she watched from the safety of her private world, until suddenly, her tranquil moment came crashing to a halt...

A menacing voice jolted her from her only place of solace, startling her in a familiar way. Jade stood frozen with fear, and reluctant to turn, as she knew the monster who lurked behind her. "Look at who we have here!" snarled the angry voice. Then forcing herself to turn, Jade found herself standing face to face with Rilee, the meanest girl in school. "What are you doing here?" Jade dared herself to ask. Ignoring the question, Rilee pressed her contorted face closer to Jade's, and began her ruthless taunt. "What's the matter, Jade? Are you scared of the little dogs?" she asked. Her mockery shook Jade to the core. She tried to defend herself, but the words caught in her throat, as it was bully who instilled indescribable terror, not the dogs. Standing before Jade, Rilee continued her slow approach. Wisps of hair fell from her sloppy ponytail, while long strands hung low over her angry scowl, casting her in a hostile light. Jade instinctively stepped back, forbidding herself to scream, while the witchy presence loomed before her. With her back against the wall. she watched as Rilee inched closer, wearing a sinister grin. "I'm going to tell everybody what a big baby you are for being afraid of the itty-bitty dogs." Rilee said. Jade looked up at her accuser, daring herself to take a stand. A potshot to Rilee's nose might work, she thought, but it might further enrage the tyrant standing before her. So, instead, Jade kept silent, while Rilee stood close, spewing her needling words. The heat of her breath, blasted against Jade's face, causing her to squint, while droplets of spittle, landed against her cheeks. With a swipe of her shirtsleeve, Jade wiped her skin dry, as she stood backed against the wall, silently, begging for mercy...

Suddenly, out of nowhere, Lilly came charging at Rilee's feet. Harnessed in her wheelie, the little dog's stance appeared angry and bold, as her curled lip revealed a long row of sharp teeth. Doing her best to look ferocious, Lilly loomed before the bully, ready to charge. Frozen with fear, Rilee dared not move, for to do so, would mean a certain dog attack, she thought. Looking down at the seemingly savage animal, Rilee begged for help. "Jade, get it away from me." she cried. Jade smiled to herself, as she knew the dog was of no real danger. Meanwhile, Lilly inched closer. "Leave Jade alone!" she shouted, but to Rilee's human ear, Lilly's words carried the sound of a vicious barking dog. Shaken by the unexpected threat, Rilee backed herself against the wall, as Lilly continued her angry attack-dog facade. Jade laughed to herself, knowing that Lilly didn't have a mean bone in her body. As she watched Rilee tremble with fear, a sleeping confidence began to awaken, for she knew then, the tables were turned. A sly smile spread across Jade's face, as she walked up to the bully. Looking her square in the eye, she spoke six simple words, freeing her from months of suffering. "Don't mess with me, ever again." Dumfounded by Jade's new-found courage, Rilee was rendered speechless. Then taking advantage of her opportunity, Jade made sure Rilee knew she meant business. Her eyes were no longer full of fear, as her look was one of empowerment, and self-confidence. "What's the matter, Rilee? Are you scared of the itty-bitty dog?" Jade asked, throwing back the bully's mocking words. Satisfied she'd made her point, Jade backed away, and watched Rilee bolt out of sight.

After Lilly's Oscar-winning performance, Jade was sure the bully wouldn't be coming around to bother her anymore. Rilee was on the run and didn't look back. Jade laughed to herself at such a sight, then turned her attention back to Lilly, but the little dog was gone. Puzzled by her sudden disappearance, she assumed Lilly ran off to play. Chaos ensued all around her with kids and dogs running amok, the entire gym-class was fast becoming one comical mishap after another. Meanwhile, Cody seemed to be enjoying every minute of the high-spirited mayhem, until he overheard the police officer and gym-teacher talking. Shaken by what they said, he ran to Jade in a panic. "We have to do something! Mister Alan just called the dog-catcher!" "Oh no! Cody, are you sure?" "Yup. I just heard the cops tell Mister B and J.C. that Animal Control is on the way!" Looking around, they could see kids and dogs enjoying their playful run, oblivious to what was about to happen next...

The situation seemed hopeless, but Jade wasn't about to give up without a fight. "Cody, we have to find a way to save the dogs!" she hollered, over the noise. Welcoming the challenge, Cody began to devise his bold and daring rescue. "It'll be okay, Jade. Now, listen carefully. I have an idea, but you'll have to trust me on this." he said, looking her in the eye. Without questioning his plan, Jade gave her nod of approval, and in an instant, Cody took off running and disappeared into the crowd. Jade knew then, her classmate was on a mission. But as bad luck would have it, she looked up to see, the dog-catcher had already arrived. Filled with dread, she watched the looming figure of a man, standing in the opposite doorway. The sun was at his back, creating a darkened silhouette. The faceless monster stood with his tools of the trade at the ready. In one hand, he clutched a long pole with a metal loop attached to the end, and in the other, he gripped a large nylon net. Knowing things were about to get ugly, Jade looked around for Cody, but he was nowhere in sight.

Meanwhile, standing at the opposite end of the gym, Corey was speaking with Brenden and Jeremy, when they noticed the dog-officer had arrived. "Hey, look who's here to save the day!" Brenden said, jokingly, noticing the dog-catcher. Corey looked up to see the old-timer standing there. "What's Richie doing here? I thought he retired ages ago." he said. Jeremy took one look at the old man, and knew the word, *retirement* was an understatement. "Corey, if you ask me, that poor old guy looks more nursing-home ready, if anything." he joked. Brenden couldn't resist a chuckle, despite his frustration. "Well, this should at least be interesting, if nothing else." he said, trying to keep a straight face. It was then, the three men, walked across the gym and greeted the old man at the door. Corey was first to speak. "Good morning, Richie. What are you doing, still working? I thought you submitted your retirement papers." he said, looking puzzled. Rich looked up, smiling through broken teeth. "I guess you just can't keep a good man down." he said, standing there, wearing a wrinkled jump-suit with food stains smeared down the front. Wisps of silvery hair curled up from underneath his time-worn cap sitting flat atop his head. The distinct odor of stale, tobacco smoke, lingered on his clothes as he bit down on the stub of a cigar, causing hard lines at the corner of his eyes, lending him an expression of a continual squint. His bulging belly, pushed hard against his clothes, suggestive that he never missed a meal, while food remnants clinging to his scraggly beard, added to his disheveled look. Rendered speechless, the three men stood back, and watched as old Rich, began his clumsy attempts to do his job.

Meanwhile, Cody was finalizing his plan when Jade found him standing at the far wall. She was shaken and out of breath. "There you are. I was looking all over for you." she said. "Calm down, Jade. Things will turn out okay, but just so you know, I'm about to stir things up a little around here. Are you with me on this?" he asked, searching her eyes for any doubt. Jade knew there was no time to waste and was willing to go along with whatever her classmate was planning. "Okay, Cody. But I'm getting just a little nervous. The dog-catcher looks like he means business." she said, looking across the gym.

Following her gaze, Cody spotted old Rich, standing at the opposite doorway. He was armed with an oversized net, wearing a look of determination, eager to snag the first dog who ran past. Oliver and Tino were the first to get caught in his netted trap. Caught by surprise, the two panicked dogs frantically worked to free themselves from the nylon webbing. Pierre could see that his brothers needed help... Running full force, he aimed for the small space between the dog-catcher's legs, nearly knocking him to the floor. Rich fought to keep his balance, while the pudgy poodle ran circles around his feet. Meanwhile, Clyde could see that Pierre was in a tight spot, and instantly ran to his aid. Feeling brave, he began tugging at the old man's trousers, causing him to fall on his backside. As Richie struggled to get to his feet, Champ bolted over and pinned him flat against the gymnasium floor. Lilly immediately saw her opportunity, and wheeled herself over his mountainous belly, and balanced herself on top, causing the entire gym-class to roar with laughter. Meanwhile, Corey, Jeremy and Brenden watched in disbelief.

12 *On the Road Again*

PERCHED ON THE WINDOWSILL, SASSY gazed outside, hopelessly awaiting the dog's safe return. She figured, it wouldn't be long before Heidi noticed them missing, and there was no doubt in her mind, the dogs would eventually find themselves in a heap of trouble. So, it was then, Sassy decided it was time to take matters into her own paws. Meanwhile, Buddy and Buster had already lost interest in the dog's recent break from the yard, and decided to indulge in a mid-morning snack. Settling next to a bowl of freshly poured kibble, the hungry duo began crunching on the fish flavored morsels. Appalled by their gluttony, Sassy watched them devourer almost every crumb. Then, without warning, a quick swipe of her paw, sent the bowl of kibble sliding, clear across the floor, causing her brothers to nearly jump out of their skins. "Hey! What did you do that for?" Buddy asked, with a mouthful of food. Buster was just as dumbfounded. Standing before them, Sassy wore a look that screamed, I mean business. "Okay, boys, now that I have your undivided attention, I need to make an announcement." she said. "Oh, come on, Sassy. Can't this wait until after we eat?" Buddy asked. Sassy shook her head. "Nope. I need your help, now. So, you two better pay close attention to what I'm about to say. Here's the thing, it doesn't look like the dogs will make it back anytime soon. So, as the superior specie, it'll be up to us to initiate a search and bring them home." she explained. Buster shuddered at the idea. A seat on the sunny windowsill was about as much adventure the skittish cat could handle. "No, I'm good, Sassy. I'll just stay right here and let you and Buddy handle it." he said. Sassy shook her head. "Don't think for one second, that you can weasel out of this one. Buster, you're coming with us whether you like it or not." "Oh really, Sassy? Give me just one good reason why I should participate in your hair-brained idea." With that, the bossy cat marched up to him, placing her clenched paw, firmly underneath his chin. "I'll give you five good reasons why you're coming with me, Buster." she said, looking him square in the eye. Meanwhile, Buddy sat back watching and figured, it wouldn't be long before Sassy offered him a fistful of motivation too. So, it was then, he suggested a more level-headed approach to the problem. "Sassy, I was thinking, maybe we should just tell Heidi the truth." Sassy shot him a look. "The truth? You want us to tell her the truth? Are you out of your mind, Buddy?" We can't just walk up to her and say, Hi Heidi. It sure is a nice day. Oh, by the way, your dogs are missing." "Sassy, that's not exactly how I envisioned telling her, but yes, just telling her the truth would be our best bet." Refusing to take no for an answer, Sassy boldly pushed open the door, and marched outside with Buddy and Buster reluctantly following behind her. It was then, the three mischievous cats began their dangerous trek across town, and pursued a search for the missing dogs...

13 Cats Meet Dog

THE SLEEPY SHIH TZU DOZED at the front stoop of Henderson's Café. Rays of sunshine streamed through the blooming branches of a young maple tree, offering the perfect combination of sun and shade. Wrapping herself in a ball with her nose tucked under her paws, Gizzy allowed herself to drift into a peaceful slumber. It was there, each day she'd patiently await the return of her beloved human. Edgar and Gizzy were inseparable. The little dog acquainted well with her human's daily routine. Each and every morning, Edgar could be found sitting at the counter, just inside Henderson's Cafe, sipping on his coffee and reading the daily news. And all the while, his little dog was content to snoozing in her favorite sunny spot, just outside the door... As she lay sleeping, a gentle breeze blew through fine wisps of her hair, hanging low over her sleepy eyes. The tip of her tongue peeked from the front of her mouth, while her fluffy ears hung like ponytails at the sides of her sleeping face. An underbite added to her adoring looks, while streams of sunshine sprinkling down upon her face, caused a sleepy squint. There, she was content to wait for her person, as she pulled her tired eyes closed, and fell deeper into a peaceful slumber..

Meanwhile, the cats were making their way down Main Street. They hadn't traveled very far when they stumbled upon the sleeping shih-tzu. "Maybe she saw which way the dogs were going." Buddy said, keeping to a whisper. The idea of disturbing her seemed rude, he thought, but that didn't stop Sassy from boldly rousing the sleeping pooch. "Excuse me, little dog, but are you awake?" Sassy asked, in a raised tone, knowing well, Gizzy was far off in the land of dreams. Buster shuddered at his sister's audacity. "Sassy, are you sure you should be waking her? After all, she could be a vicious attack dog or something." Sassy burst with laughter. "Are you kidding me, Buster? Whoever heard of a ferocious shih-tzu?" Startled by the sound of Sassy's belly laughs, Gizzy popped her head. Then, noticing the trio of cats standing over her, the pint-sized dog jumped to her paws, causing the cats to startle in return. "Oh, hello little doggy. I hope we didn't scare you." Sassy said, in a sugary voice. "Allow me to introduce myself. My name is, Sassy. Here with me are my brother's, Buster and Buddy. We're out here trying to find our friends, and wondered if maybe you noticed which way they were heading." Without giving Gizzy a moment to answer, Sassy began a mile-a-minute description of the dogs they were looking for. "You may have spotted Clyde, a shih-tzu just like yourself. He would have been traveling with Pierre, a medium sized poodle about yea high." she said, gesturing with her paw. "Or maybe it was Oliver who caught your eye. He's a bit lanky, sporting long graying fur. He would have been carrying, Tino, an itsy-bitsy, white poodle on his back. Has anyone fitting those descriptions pass by?" Gizzy did her best to take in everything the fast-talking cat said. A sight like that would surely be hard to miss, she thought, but then again, she'd been sleeping. The little dog shook her head. "Sassy, I'm really sorry, but I didn't notice anyone matching those descriptions. If you'd like, I could help you find your friends." she offered in a soft voice, matching her petite size. Delighted by Gizzy's proffer, Sassy quickly accepted, instantly sending Buster into a state of panic. "Sassy, are you out of your mind? We can't take her with us." "I don't see why not, Buster. What's the big deal? And besides, we could really use her help." "Sassy, we can't afford to lose another dog. It's just too risky." "Buster, just stop it. You're worrying for nothing. We won't lose Gizzy." It wasn't like the other cats to argue with their bossy sister, but Buster knew he was right. "Sassy, will you please just listen to me for a second? All I'm saying is, her human will eventually come out of that coffee-shoppe, and I'm pretty sure he won't be happy if his dog isn't here, waiting for him when he does." Buddy nodded in agreement. "He's right, Sassy." It wasn't like him to take sides, but he knew his brother made a good point. Then, realizing she was outnumbered, Sassy suggested an idea. "Well, if that's how you guys really feel, maybe we should just let the little dog decide whether or not she stays or goes." Keeping to her sweet tone, Sassy turned to Gizzy and worked her persuading powers. "So, listen here, little dog. My brothers have no idea what they're talking about. We'll be back, way before your human is finished with his coffee and newspaper. And besides, he'll probably never even notice you're missing." Wrapping her paw around Gizzy, Sassy pulled her close and continued her sweet-talking facade. "I'm sorry, sweetie, but I didn't catch your name." Looking to Sassy, Gizzy beamed with pride. "Who, me? Well, my name is, Gizzy, but human sometimes calls me, Gaga." Sassy knew time was running short and was in no mood for chit-chat. "Listen to me, Gizzy or Gaga, or whatever your name is. Don't listen to my brothers. Those two worry about everything, and besides, we could really use your help. So, what do you say, Gaga? Are you gonna to just stay here and sleep the day away, or are you gonna make yourself useful, and help us find our friends?" Gizzy thought for a moment. She didn't want to disobey her human by leaving without his knowledge, but the idea of helping the cats seemed a good deed. Feeling conflicted, little Gizzy thought long and hard about what to do. Meanwhile, Sassy's patience was growing thin. "So, Gizzy, what's it gonna be? Are you coming with us or not?" she asked, losing her sweet tone. Pushed into making a hasty decision, Gizzy agreed to join the cats in their search for the missing dogs. "Yes, Sassy, you can count me in." Overjoyed with her successful recruitment,

Sassy patted Gizzy on the back and began to lead the way. "That a girl! You won't regret this, Goo-goo, um... I mean, Gaga."

So, it was then, sweet Gizzy joined forces with the cats and courageously made her way down the busy road. Oblivious of the prevailing dangers, the little dog's bravery would soon be put to the test as her daring adventure continued...

14 *Clear the Gym*

T HE GYMNASIUM FAST BECAME A free-for-all with kids and dogs running in every direction. Happy sounds of laughter and running footsteps echoed throughout the wide-open space. It all seemed like fun and games, until Lilly witnessed Oliver and Tino's close call with the dog-catcher's net. It was then, she had a change of heart, and quickly realized the dangers her brothers faced by following her to school that day. Surrounded by the crowd, they stood before her expecting praise for their efforts. Tino sat tall upon Oliver's back, reminiscent of a warrior atop his horse, prepared for battle. His courage brought a smile to Lilly's face, for she knew, the old dog's bravery, was greater than his tea-cup size. And so, concerned for her brother's safety, Lilly lashed out, knowing they were in danger. "What are you guys doing here?" she asked. Her harsh tone matched her angry look. Stunned by Lilly's reaction, Oliver stood before her, fighting back the tears. All he wanted, was to see his sister home where she belonged. "Lilly, don't you understand? We came all this way because we were worried about you." "Well, I'm totally fine, Ollie. You guys shouldn't have come." "But we had no idea you were all right. We were only trying to help." With that, Oliver turned away in an attempt to hide his crying eyes. Realizing she overreacted, Lilly felt terrible for lashing out at him. It was plain to see, her brothers had her best interest at heart, and the way they risked their own safety out of concern for hers, spoke volumes. So, it was then, she began her humbled apologies. "Oliver, I'm really sorry for getting so upset with you. I didn't mean to hurt your feelings, and I know you guys were only trying to help." Hanging her head in shame, Lilly hoped that her brother would forgive her outburst. "It's okay, Lilly. I know you didn't mean it." "Thanks Ollie. You see, what started out as a quest to satisfy my curiosity, turned into something so much more." Lilly's voice took on a solemn tone as she spoke of her chance meeting with Jade earlier that morning. Sensing his sister's sorrow, Oliver couldn't understand why making a new friend would cause so much sadness. Meanwhile, Clyde approached, and could see his sister struggling with emotion. "What's the matter, Lilly? Why do you look like you lost your best friend?" he asked. Her glistening eyes revealed a deepened sadness, as her thoughts trailed back to those she once loved and lost, while living in Thailand. Lilly was no stranger to painful goodbyes, and always dared herself to love again despite a broken heart. Her chance meeting with Jade, that day, blossomed into a special friendship, and the mere thought of never seeing her again, filled her with unimaginable heartbreak. It was then, Lilly looked hopelessly across the crowded gymnasium, but Jade was nowhere in sight. So, it was true, just as Clyde said, Lilly seemed to have lost her new best friend.

Things were growing wildly out of control inside the gym, and although Lilly's heart's desire was to find Jade, she knew getting her brothers home would have to take precedent. How a simple trip to school became so complicated was beyond her, she thought. So, it was then, she began the task of implementing some damage control strategies in hopes to restore the normalcy of everybody's day. Giving the dogcatcher the slip would be an easy fix, judging by his clumsy display. Surely, Mister Alan would calm down once the dogs cleared the gym. Corey and Champ would likely return to the road- detail, and Brenden's gym class would once and for all, resume its normal fashion. In the end, Jeremy could eventually get back to counseling his students, and with any luck, the dogs would make it home before anyone noticed them missing. Unbeknownst to Lilly, the cats were on their way, and with Gizzy tagging along, the situation was about to get worse. So, just when she thought she had a chance of fixing the terrible mess they were in, Gizzy and the cats were about to make the scene...

Meanwhile, Cody was on the other side of the gym, chomping at the bit. More than ever, the young boy was ready to initiate his daring plan. But as soon as Jade saw what he was about to do, she instinctively grabbed at his hand. "Cody, are you out of your mind? You can't pull the fire-alarm!" "Well, do you have a better idea?" he asked, with a sneaky glimmer in his eye. "But you'll cause a panic." Jade said, looking confused. "Yup! That's the plan." "But, why Cody? I don't understand." "Jade, listen to me. It won't be long before the dog-catcher gets lucky enough to snag the dogs. We need to create a diversion in order to clear the gym, and the fire-alarm is our only hope." Judging by her worried look, Cody could tell that his classmate preferred a more subdued approach. "Jade, we have no other choice. So, unless you have a better idea, you need to let go of my hand so I can get this party started." "But, Cody..." she started to say. Then, cutting her off mid-sentence, Cody began to explain his risky plan. Feeling conflicted, Jade thought for a moment, before finally, dropping her hand from his, thus allowing him to pull the switch. In an instant, the screaming alarm, echoed throughout gymnasium, causing the level of chaos to skyrocket out of control. A wave of panic spread throughout the school, as students poured from the building at every exit. Caught by surprise, Brenden tried in vain to call order to the panicked group, but the stampede of students rushing past, nearly knocked him to the ground. Meanwhile, Jeremy did his best to calm the rowdy crowd, but his voice paled in comparison to the boisterous bunch. Corey was nearby, working to ensure everybody's safe exit, completely unaware the fire department was on its way. And through it all, Lilly remained harnessed in her wheel-cart, seemingly unfazed by the chaos ensuing around her. Standing amidst the crowd, she searched the faces of every child who ran past, but, it was Jade, who she was looking for...

15 Engine One Ladder Two

A LULL IN EMERGENCY CALLS offered a much-needed respite for the men and women of engine company eighteen. As a firefighter on duty, sleepless nights and interrupted meals were considered the norm. But for this dedicated crew, responding to emergencies was nothing more than any average day on the job.

Finally, a little downtime, Elliot thought, plopping into one of the empty recliner chairs, lining the front of the wide-screen TV. His gaping yawn spoke volumes as a need for sleep left him feeling drained. He figured, snagging a little shut-eye before the next call would be supreme. The last twenty-four-hour shift was killer, plaguing him with pure exhaustion. His military-style boots pulled hard at his legs like cast-iron anchors locked to his feet. He was no stranger to laborious work, but on this day, Elliot found himself struggling to keep up with the back-to-back emergency runs. His youthfulness lent him a naturally lean physique, but even so, he enjoyed working in some running miles during an off-shift. With his earbuds in place, he'd lose himself in private thoughts, while the rhythm of his favorite upbeat music, pounded at his ears. But when the effects of the previous shift took an exhausting toll, the young rookie felt depleted of his seemingly, endless supply of energy. Finally, able to pull his sleepy eyes closed, Elliot surrendered to his need for sleep. Allowing a peaceful slumber to take hold, he began a slow drift, deeper into an ocean of dreams. A tranquil and soothing buoyancy enveloped his weary body and carried him away, until a sudden burst of laughter erupting from the galley, landed him on the hard shore of wakefulness. Startled by the unexpected noise, his sleepy eyes blinked open, soon realizing his time of rest would be short-lived. Finally, deciding to join the crew, Elliot pushed his fatigued body from the overstuffed chair, and made his way down the short hallway, leading to the kitchen. His nose lifted to the aroma of freshly baked pizza, wafting past, instantly sparking his appetite. "Hey, guys." he said, with a sleepy rasp. Barely awake, he entered the snug dining area and planked himself at the table in one of the empty chairs. "Well look at who we have here. Sleeping Beauty has decided to join us." Brian teased. Remembering his days as a rookie, Brian knew Elliot would eventually adjust to the grueling schedule a firefighter endured. "Very funny, Brian." Elliot said, with a sleepy grin. Everyone appreciated Brian's good-natured humor and never took offense to his razzing.

As a newcomer to the department, Elliot was a quick learner and never hesitated to go out of his way to help others. And for that, he was well liked. Adding to his appeal, his dazzling, hazel eyes, and wide smile could light up any room. He was never one to primp over his appearance because his good looks came naturally. His sandy, blond locks were usually buzzed short, but a few missed barber appointments left him with a little more on top than he wanted. On that day, his sleepy eyes were mere slits, revealing only a hint of their masculine beauty. Despite his extreme exhaustion, Elliot joined the crew, and readied himself for a something to eat. Realizing that getting sleep would have to wait, he figured, there'd at least be some time for a quick slice of pizza before the next run. But as bad luck would have it, his food would have to wait too, as another emergency call sounded from the loud-speaker, snapping him from his sleepy fog. The attention-getting tone rang throughout the station before the call was dispatched. *"Attention ladder one, engine one and rescue two. Respond to sixty-eight Robinson Ave for a three-alarm call to the Alan Taylor Middle School. Attention alarm! Alan Taylor middle school... Time out 13:22."* The dispatcher's voice echoed throughout the firehouse while the crew sprang into action. Elliot climbed aboard the fifty-foot tiller truck. Steering from the rear with his headset in place, he communicated to the driver at the front. With the flick of a switch, the colossal machine roared to life with its swirling beacons of light and powerful engine. Pungent fumes permeated throughout the apparatus room, as the fleet of trucks roared to life. The screaming sirens created a cacophony that echoed loudly within the tall walls of the brick building. One by one, the entire fleet rolled from the station. Sitting tall in his seat, Elliot skillfully, negotiated every turn throughout the city streets as he continued his fast drive to the school. Suddenly, he began to feel an intermittent thump against his boot. Finally, after a nagging curiosity took hold, his split-second glance below the dash revealed the unexpected sight. To his utter shock, sitting there, peeking from the darkness, was Gizzy, the pint size, shih-tzu from Henderson's Bakery.

16 Cats to the "Rescue"

T HE FLOW OF TRAFFIC PARTED, allowing for the speeding emergency vehicles to pass. Blaring sirens ripped through the air, catching the attention of onlookers from all around. When the call was dispatched to the Alan Taylor Middle School, the crew quickly sprang into action. Elliot manned the tiller, while Brian took his seat at the wheel in the ambulance. Racing to the scene, both men prepared for yet another crisis an ordinary day on the job would behold, only to discover, this emergency run would be far from ordinary.

Driving at top speeds, Brian maneuvered the ambulance throughout the city blocks. Just behind his seat, an empty stretcher remained locked in place. Earlier that day, the neatly dressed cot appealed to the cats when their quest to find Lilly became a tiring task. At the time, a quick catnap seemed a good idea, but they never anticipated the ambulance to take off, on a high-speed trek across town. And so, the three panicked felines woke up to a screaming siren and nauseating thrill-ride they wouldn't soon forget.

"Tell me again, whose bright idea was this?" Sassy was fuming. Getting trapped inside the ambulance with her brothers was not what she had planned. Buster was terrified to be on such a ride. The panic-stricken cat gripped the rail of the stretcher like his life depended on it. Meanwhile, Buddy fared no better... Sitting wide-eyed and fuzzed out, his splayed claws dug into anything he could get his paws on, as he too, sat at the mercy of the turbulent ride.

The blaring siren and roar of the engine, fast became the perfect combination for head-banging noise for the trio of cats, who sat trapped and afraid, inside the speeding ambulance. With no escape, they huddled close, unsure of their dreadful fate. "We're all gonna to die!" Buster cried out loud. The faint-hearted feline, clung to the cot, sure that his life was about to come to an untimely end. "Get ahold of yourself, Buster!" Sassy shouted. The noise of the siren muffled her voice as she continued her angry rant. "This van ride won't be the end of you, but I will be, if you don't knock it off!" Meanwhile, Buddy ducked in the corner. Although he was afraid to be on such a ride, the wrath of Sassy, scared him even more. So, in effort to stay below her radar, he suffered in silence, hoping for the horrifying tour across town to end. Suddenly, dawning on him, he noticed that Gizzy was nowhere in sight. He was sure, she was right behind him when they climbed into the ambulance earlier that day. Suddenly, hit with a wave of panic, the dreadful task of telling Sassy that the little dog was lost, loomed before him. But without much choice, he mustered the courage to break the bad news. "Sassy, do you have a minute? Because if not, this can totally wait." he began. Turning, she gave him a puzzled look. "Of course, I have a minute. In fact, I probably have all day. In case you haven't noticed, we're trapped like rats in the back of this horror-show on wheels, and it doesn't look like we'll be getting out anytime soon." Her voice, drenched with sarcasm, lead him to believe, she wasn't going to like what he was about to say. "Sassy, I don't like being the bearer of bad news, but it appears that Gizzy is sort of missing." His body tensed as he anticipated her explosive reaction. Sure enough, Sassy looked at him with eyes wide with anger, as she spoke through clenched teeth. "Buddy, what do you mean, Gizzy is *sort of missing*?" Buddy knew there was no turning back. So, he reluctantly, continued his true confession. "Sassy, I hate to admit it but, Gizzy is missing, gone without a trace. She's not back here." "Buddy, where did she go?" "Well, if I knew that, then she wouldn't be missing now, would she?" Sassy was livid. "Buddy, how could you lose her?" "I didn't lose her, Sassy. Gizzy just disappeared." "Buddy, are you out of your mind? Dogs don't just disappear into thin air." "Well, Gizzy did." he said. Meanwhile, Buster was listening, and came to his brother's defense. "Sassy, now don't freak out or anything, but remember, we tried to warn you, bringing Gizzy with us was a bad idea." "Oh, I see how it is, Buster. You guys are trying to pin the missing pooch on me." "Sassy, will you please just calm down for a second? Nobody is pinning anything on anyone." "Calm down? How do you expect me to calm down after Buddy just informed me that Gizzy is amongst the missing? Oh, and let's not forget we're trapped inside this ridiculous hospital on wheels, all because you guys thought it was a good place to take a nap." The boys knew, there'd be no winning with their sister. So, they sat in silence, and endured her angry rant. Meanwhile, Brian was up front, continuing his fast drive to the school. Turning an ear, he picked up, on sounds coming from the back, until finally, dismissing them as a byproduct of his overtired mind. Then realizing they were nearly discovered, the cats ducked behind his seat, doing their best to remain hidden. "Don't even breath." Sassy warned. "So, what do we do now?" Buster asked, keeping to a whisper. "We wait for the ambulance to stop." "Is that the best you can come up with?" "Well, it's not like we can just tap the driver on the shoulder and say, excuse me sir, but this is our stop." "Don't you think I know that, Sassy? I just don't think I can take much more of this heave-worthy drive across town." Feeling sicker than sick, Buster was sure it was the end of the road for him. "Listen to me, Buster. Sooner or later this moving nightmare will stop, and when it does, we'll simply jump out." Neither, Buster nor Buddy felt very reassured. "Okay Sassy, but even if we manage to escape this death-trap without going belly-up, Gizzy will still be missing." Buddy reminded. "Well, then I guess we'll just have to add her to our list of lost dogs to find." Sassy said. But little did they know, Gizzy was on a thrill-ride of her own, hidden beneath the dash of the speeding tiller-truck, well on her way to the school.

17 Schools Out

AWAVE OF PANIC SPREAD throughout the school, causing a mad rush of students to pour from every exit. The emptying hallways reverberated with the shrill of the fire-alarm, creating massive confusion throughout the building. Kids could be seen running from all sides, with their hands pressed against their ears, trying to escape the ear-piercing noise. Pulling up to the school, Brian instantly noticed the parking lot swarming with people. Elliot wasn't far behind driving the tiller-truck. It's wailing siren and winding engine could be heard for blocks, until finally, rolling to a stop behind the parked ambulance. The fifty-foot truck remained at an idle with its swirling beacons of light, signaling an emergency inside the school...

Jumping from his seat, Brian made his way to the back of the ambulance. Stopping short, he looked up to see Elliot climbing from the tiller with a pint-sized dog in his arms.

"Well, look at what we have here. I didn't know the department had a new mascot." he mused, with a pat to Gizzy's head. Feeling exhausted, Elliot was in no mood for his co-worker's jokes. "Not funny, Brian." "So, what's up with the dog?" Brian asked. "It beats me. The poor thing was hiding below the dash. I just happened to glance down and boom, there she was, staring up at me looking wide-eyed and scared out of her mind." Elliot said. Meanwhile, Corey had just made his way outside when he noticed Elliot and Brian, standing by the firetrucks. "Alas, the calvary has arrived." he joked, running up to them. "I see you guys found another dog." he said, spotting Gizzy. "What do you mean by *another dog*?" Elliot asked, looking puzzled. Before Corey could answer, Jeremy and Brenden ran up, catching their breath, wearing a look of defeat. Brenden's shirt, sopped with sweat, clung to his muscular physique, while Jeremy's male-model appearance, took on a more disheveled look. "Man, what the heck happened to you guys?" Brian asked, giving them a look. "We've been chasing after dogs all morning." Jeremy said, wiping his forehead. Brenden nodded in agreement. "You can say that again. My gym- class took a nosedive after a bunch of stray dogs made the scene." he said. "So, that's your big emergency? Dogs?" Elliot asked, looking annoyed. As always, Brian was quick with a joke. "Come on guys. You mean to tell me, you couldn't handle a few woof woofs all by yourselves?" "Listen, Brian. Neither one of us called the fire department over a few stray dogs." Corey explained. "We figured out that one of the kids pulled the fire-alarm, and Principal Alan was the one who dropped a dime about the dog running around the gym. But what I still don't understand is, how did the dogs from my road detail, end up here at the school? And stranger yet, Elliot just shows up with a shih-tzu he found hiding in tiller- truck. What's going on around here?" "I have no idea, Corey." Brian said, with a hint of laughter. "But one thing's for sure, this is the stuff that movies are made of. I can see it now... *Killer shih-tzu and poodles, take over the city.* Jeremy smiled, envisioning the sight. "Oh, that'd definitely, push Mister Alan over the edge. He's wound up so tight, I swear, one of these days, he'll give himself a heart-attack." he said, shaking his head." Corey agreed. "Yeah, and apparently, he's the one who called, Animal Control, but old Richie turned out to be a joke. That poor guy couldn't even catch a cold, if he tried, let alone a running pack of dogs." "Well, that's an understatement, if I ever heard one." Brenden said, remembering old Richie's clumsy display. Then noticing the gym-teacher's frustration, Brian couldn't resist another joke. "Just relax, Mister B. By tomorrow, this whole day will be just one big bad memory." he said, with a chuckle. But little did Brian know, the joke would be on him, as he was still unaware that Sassy, Buddy, and Buster, were trapped inside his ambulance, and things were about to take an unexpected turn. With three terrified cats, six runaway dogs, and two determined kids, it was anybody's guess as to what would happen next...

Meanwhile, Jade and Cody had been observing the ensuing chaos. Pandemonium spread throughout the school, causing teachers and students to pour from the building. The shrill of the alarm blasted across the grounds, but despite it all, the dog-catcher continued his lame attempts to snag any dog who ran past. Seeing this, Cody was more than ready to initiate phase two of his daring mission, but he could tell that Jade was having second thoughts. "Okay, Cody. So, what's your next brilliant idea?" she asked, in a voice riddled with sarcasm. "It's a total mad-house out there. We'll never get the dogs now." she said. The parking lot swarmed with people, and with the Police and Fire Departments involved, she was sure they were both in big trouble. "Just relax, Jade. We can handle this." "Cody, how do you expect me to relax when we just created a disaster." "No Jade. You got it all wrong. This isn't a disaster. Don't you see? We just created the perfect diversion." Jade was a bundle of nerves, and was more than ready abort the mission. It was easy to see, she was having doubts about Cody's scheme. He figured, she'd eventually calm down once he explained the next phase of his plan, but he quickly found out, he was wrong... "Cody, are you out of your mind? We can't do that!" Folding her arms in disapproval, Jade was dead-set against his outrageous idea. "But it's the best I can come up with." "Cody, you really are losing your mind. What you're suggesting will definitely land us in the principal's office, or worse." "Well, do you have a better idea?" he asked, knowing she didn't. "No, but..." she started to say, but he cut her off mid-sentence. "Jade, just listen to me. We don't have a choice. It's the only way to keep the dogs together and transport them to safety." he reasoned. The last thing either of them wanted was for any of the dogs to end up at the city pound. So, it was then, Jade talked herself into believing his idea was their only option. She was falling fast from her familiar comfort zone, but in the end, she agreed, and went along with his daredevil plan...

The ambulance sat parked, idling in front of the school. Meanwhile, Corey and the others stood at the back, lost in conversation. Jade and Cody could see that J.C. and Mister B were busy speaking with the police and fire department, so it was then, they made their move... They began their sneaky approach, ducked low, tiptoeing on either side of the ambulance. Doing their best remain unnoticed, Cody quietly pulled open the driver's side door, and took a seat behind the wheel, just as Jade crept onto the passenger side. Knowing they were about to cross a dangerous line, she pulled the seatbelt across her lap, and prepared to carry out their brazen and foolhardy act, all in a desperate attempt to save the dogs. Without a word, she sat focusing her gaze straight ahead. Noticing her silence, Cody looked to her, and wondered what thoughts she might be churning. "Jade are you okay?" he asked, sitting on the driver's side. Keeping silent, her blank stare suggested she was miles away, lost in deep and private thoughts. "Earth to Jade." Cody said, prompting an answer. Breaking from her trance, she looked to him without uttering a single word. "Jade are you all right?" he asked again, searching her eyes for an answer. Finally, giving him a slight nod, Cody took his que and hit the gas. In an instant, the ambulance sped off like a shot, and fish-tailed out of sight.

18 Back at the Ranch

HEIDI RELISHED THE TIME OF year when Mother Nature awakened from her long winter's nap. Soothing to the soul, the delicate scent of blossoming lilacs wafted past her open window. Spring had sprung and her mornings were now full of the promise of new and wonderful things. The sunlit sky created the perfect backdrop for a late spring morning. Golden rays streamed down onto the yard, created ideal basking spots for her sleeping dogs. Oblivious to their disappearance, she lifted the windows, inviting in some of nature's perfect air. Drawing in deep breaths, she relished the delicate aroma of blossoms bathing in the tepid air just outside her door. Suddenly, overcome with a feeling that something wasn't quite right, she turned a listening ear... The dogs seemed unusually quiet, she thought. Thinking it best to check on her pack, she began to make her way outside, until something on the news, caught her eye, stopping her dead in her tracks...

19 Coffee and Donuts

HENDERSON'S CAFÉ WAS BUSTLING WITH its usual breakfast crowd. Just inside, Edgar sat over a cup of steaming, hot coffee, while the soothing aroma of freshly brewed pots, permeated throughout the quaint, breakfast nook. Rows of cream-filled pastries, adorning rainbow-colored sprinkles, lined the back wall, tempting, and pleasing to the eye. Standing at the back, the short-order cook worked feverishly, filling orders of flapjacks, and home-fries, to hungry patrons on the go. Edgar relished the home-style vibe of his favorite breakfast place. There, he'd sit at the counter alongside a few of his closest friends with his coffee in hand, and newspaper spread before him. All the while, his beloved dog, Gizzy was content to wait just outside, dozing in her favored sunny spot.

Just like clockwork, Edgar's lifelong friend, Benjamin, entered the diner, and joined him at the counter. Noticing Ed was deep onto his morning read, Ben started with his usual attempt at humor. "Morning, Eddie. You looking to see if you made the obits yet?" he jokingly, asked. With a laugh, Edgar was quick with his reply. "Ha! No way, Benny. These old bones ain't going anywhere, just yet." he said, keeping to his paper. Meanwhile, Anne stood behind the counter, sporting an apron, and a smile, always at the ready with a coffee-pot in hand, and a pen tucked behind her ear, ready to take your order. "What can I get you, Ben? she asked, pouring him a cup." "I'll take just the coffee, Annie. Thanks" "No bagel or toast?" "Nah. I'll just stick with the coffee for now." "Okay, Hun. Let me know if you change your mind." she said, then, turning to Edgar. "How about you, Ed. You all set?" "I'm good, Annie. Thanks though." Anne was the heart and soul of Henderson's Bakery and Diner. Each and every morning, she'd make her rounds from table to table, mingling with her regulars, while she busily took their orders of home-fries and scrambled eggs. Always packing a crowd, the sounds of chatter filled the cozy nook, as the busboy busily worked to clear tables, clanking dirty plates into his tote, while a long line of hungry patrons waited to take a seat. Mounted just above the counter, the television came alive with a pair of smiling, news anchors, reporting the daily events. Meanwhile, the men sat side by side, Edgar with his newspaper, and Benjamin with his eye, glued to the set. All seemed mundane, until something caught Ben's attention. "Eddie, check it out. You gotta see this." he said, pointing to the TV. Pulling from his paper, Edgar looked up to see a harried news-anchor, reporting live from the Alan Taylor Middle School.

She stood surrounded by the boisterous crowd, clutching her microphone, and doing her best to keep to her feet, while kids and dogs ran circles around her. "Looks like there could be trouble at the school." Edgar said, taking a sip of his coffee. Nodding his head, Benjamin turned an ear to catch the full report. "I think I heard her say something about a dog." he said. As if on que, Lilly raced by with her wheels in tow, nearly knocking the reporter to the ground. Shocked by such a sight, Ben jumped to his feet. "Holy cow! Did you see that, Eddie?" he asked, pointing up at the TV. "I sure did, Benny." Edgar said, smiling to himself. Champ was next to make his television debut. The oversized hound, rushed past the reporter, barking and howling like a beagle on the prowl.

Oliver came next, weaving through the crowd with Tino riding high on his back like a rodeo cowboy. The two made their way around the schoolyard, until something caught Oliver's ear, causing him to spook. He frantically kicked and bucked, while old, Tino held on with all his might. Clyde came next, digging through lunch-bags, as the ever-hungry, shih-tzu was always on the prowl for a tasty snack. Meanwhile, Pierre stood amidst the mayhem. Emergency vehicles scattered about with their swirling beacons of blue and yellow, strobed against his black fur, lending him the distinctive look of a disco-dog. Edgar was in hysterics at such a sight. Tears of laughter rolled down his hilly cheeks, and his eyes grew onto mere slits behind his bifocal glasses. Pulling a handkerchief from his shirt pocket, he blotted his watery eyes in an attempt to gain his composure. Then suddenly, his laughing-fit came crashing to a halt when his eye caught the jaw-dropping sight. There, in front of him on live television, was his own precious dog caught up in the chaos. "Gizzy!" he shouted, jumping to his feet. His heart dropped like a rock, when he realized his beloved pet was no longer outside, waiting for him. Filled with panic, Edgar bolted from the diner as fast as he could, and within seconds, he was in his car, slamming it in gear. "Don't worry, Gaga! I'm coming to save you!" he hollered, as his car sped out of sight.

20 *The Reunion*

THE SHRILL OF THE ALARM rang-out across the schoolyard. Panicked students fled the building and swarmed the lot, while teachers did their best to calm the frantic group. Surrounded by the mayhem, Lilly soon realized, her bus-ride to school, offered more than she bargained for. Never in her wildest dreams, did she imagine her day would involve the police and fire departments. Filled with worry, she stood amidst the chaos, knowing that she was the cause of it all.

Meanwhile, caught up in the maelstrom, Gizzy found herself sitting alone and afraid. Her decision to help the cats didn't work out as she planned, and she was beginning to worry about how she'd ever find her way back to Edgar. She was missing him terribly, and knew it wouldn't be long before he noticed she was no longer waiting outside the diner. And so, Gizzy hid behind a brave facade, hoping to find a way home. Meanwhile, Lilly noticed the little shih-tzu, looking lost, and wondered who she was. So, it was then, she wheeled herself over, and began her interrogation. "Who are you and what are you doing here all by yourself?" she asked. Startled by Lilly's quick approach, Gizzy looked up in surprise. "Are you talking to me?" Gizzy asked. "Yes, little dog, I'm talking to you. So, tell me, what's your name?" Lilly demanded. "Well, my name is actually, Gizzy, but my friends just call me, Gaga." "Okay. Nice to meet you Gaga, or I mean, Gizzy. My name is, Princess Lilly, but my friends just call me, Lilly. So, enough of the small-talk. Now, Gizzy, will you please tell me what you're doing here all by yourself?" "Delighted to be in the presence of royalty, Gizzy looked adorningly at the wheel-chair bound dog standing before her. "It's very nice to meet you, Your Highness." she said, bowing her head. Although Lilly appreciated the little dog's respectful gesture, she knew there was no time to waste. "Gizzy, please just answer the question. WHAT ARE YOU DOING HERE?" Startled by Lilly's abrupt tone, Gizzy finally obliged with an answer. "I was supposed to be helping my cat friends find their missing sister, but then I sort of got lost." "Gizzy, I'm really sorry to hear that you're lost, but did you just say, you were helping your *cat* friends?" Gizzy nodded. "That's right. Three of them." Lilly was pretty sure she knew who Gizzy's cat friends were. "Tell me, Gizzy... These cat friends of yours, would you happen to remember their names?" Lilly asked, hoping to confirm her suspicions. Gizzy thought before answering... "Um, let me see. I'm pretty sure the bossy one called herself, Sassy. Oh yes, now I remember...

and the other two were, Buddy and Buster." Lilly's eyes grew wide with anger at the sound of Gizzy's answer. "I knew it! I should have known, Sassy couldn't mind her own business." she said, shaking her head. "Listen to me, Goo-goo, I mean, Gaga. I need your help. Do you know where the cats are now?" Gizzy proudly nodded. "I sure do, Lilly." she said, seemingly oblivious to the seriousness of their predicament. "Listen to me, Gaga. We're all in big trouble. I need to know, where are the cats? Where did they go, Gizzy?" Surrounded by chaos, things were beginning to look hopeless, and Lilly knew that finding three skittish felines would be nearly impossible with so many people around. She figured, they wouldn't come out of hiding until things calmed down a little. Meanwhile, Gizzy could see that Lilly was growing more anxious by the second, but figured, what she was about to tell her, would put her mind at ease. "Don't you worry about a thing, Your Highness. The cats will be just fine." she said. "Listen, Gaga. You can stop with the royalties, all right? I'm not really a princess. So, tell me, how can you be so sure the cats are okay?" "Well, last I knew, the three of them were fast asleep in that." Gizzy said, pointing to the runaway ambulance. Lilly didn't want to believe it. "You've got to be kidding me! Gizzy, please say it isn't so. Now I'll never find the cats!" Lilly cried, as she watched the ambulance disappear down the street.

Brian stood dumbfounded as his ambulance raced out of sight. "What the..." he started to say. He was at a loss for words and couldn't imagine who might be behind the wheel.

Meanwhile, Corey wasted no time. In an instant, he took off in his cruiser and was hot on the trail of the would-be thief. Then refusing to sit idle, Brian motioned for Elliot to meet him at the tiller-truck. "Brian, I hope you're not thinking, what it is, I think, you're thinking. Do you really expect to chase down the ambulance in a fifty-five foot long, tiller? Man, were talking over thirty tons of steel right here." Elliot said, slapping the side of the truck. Brian gave him a look. "Well, I really don't have a choice, Elliot." "I always knew you were out of your mind." Elliot said, shaking this head. "Ha! You think so? Well, you're the one who's crazy, if you think I'm gonna just stand back, while someone makes off with my ambulance, and takes it for a joyride across town!" "Oh, take it easy, Brian. Just let the police just do their job." "I could, but why should I let Corey have all the fun?" Shaking his head, Elliot knew there'd be no winning him. "Okay, Brian. Have it your way. Let's go before I change my mind." he said, making his way to the truck. With that, the two men climbed aboard the mighty tiller. Manning the controls, the colossal machine roared to life. Its wailing siren could be heard throughout city, as they drove from the school. Meanwhile, Jeremy and Brenden had ideas of their own. Refusing to miss any of the action, they jumped into Brenden's car, and joined the pursuit of the runaway ambulance.

Sitting behind the wheel, Cody kept a fierce eye on the road as a surge of adrenaline coursed his veins. Hitting top speeds, his passion for adventure shined in the way he drove.

Carefully calculating every turn throughout the city streets, Cody was in his glory, for in his mind, the run in the ambulance was nothing more than a true-to-life video game. Meanwhile, Jade sat quietly, staring straight ahead. Thoughts of Lilly pulled her back to their chance meeting earlier that morning. Judging by her silence, Cody could tell she miles away, drowning in a sea of deep thoughts. "What are you thinking about?" he asked, keeping his eye on the road. Concerned by her silence, he pressed for an answer. "Hey, are you okay over there? I'm talking to you." Thinking for a moment, Jade answered in a voice drenched with worry. "Cody, what if we can't find Lilly, or any of the dogs, for that matter. We can't just leave them to get hauled off to the pound." "Jade, I promise, I won't let that happen to them. And besides, I have an idea, but I'll need you to trust me on this one, okay?" he said, keeping to his driving. Jade nodded, as he went on to explain. "Okay, good. So, here's the plan... We'll backtrack to the school. Once we pull up to the lot, I'll need you to push open the rear door, and call for the dogs. With any luck, they'll hear you and come running. Once they do, just scoop them up, and pull them inside, then I'll drive them someplace safe. Easy as one, two, three." Giving him a look, Jade had doubts about his plan. "Cody, do you mind telling me, how you expect me to just, *scoop up* a pack of dogs?" "Oh, come on, Jade. It's no big deal. I'm sure you'll figure it out." "No big deal? How can you even say that? This whole situation is a big deal!" Jade said, fuming mad. "So, tell me, Cody, while

I'm back there doing all the work, what will your job be?" she asked, giving him a look. "Well, I'll be serving as lookout, of course. And besides, one of us has to drive." he said, matter-of-factly. "I have a better idea, Cody. How about, I drive, and serve as lookout, while you call for the dogs and load them?" "No way, Jade. I got this. Just leave the driving to me. You can drive, later." "Later? I don't think so, Cody. Pull over, and let me drive." "Jade, you're already driving, as in, you're driving me crazy!" "Cody, just face it. You have no idea what you're doing." "I do so, Jade. You gotta give me some, credit. I got us this far, didn't I?" "Oh, so it's credit you want? I'll give you credit, all right. Credit for getting us arrested, for taking off in an ambulance that doesn't even belong to us!" More than ever, Jade regretted agreeing to Cody's plan. "Oh, come on, Jade. We won't get arrested." he said, rolling his eyes. "Once this whole this thing is over, we'll simply explain to the police, we were saving the dogs. I'm sure they'll understand. Just calm down, Jade. Everything will turn out okay." "Cody, might I remind you, we're responsible for the false alarm that created a panic at our school. Not to mention, were riding around in a stolen ambulance, and neither one of us is even legally, old enough to drive. So, how can you just sit there, and tell me that everything will turn out okay?" Jade knew she was in way over his head. Her deep concern for the dog's safety, took precedent over her veneration for the law, caused feelings of confliction that painfully weighed on her conscience. But in the end, she decided to move forward with Cody's plan. It better pan-out, she thought, as they circled back to the school...

Just as planned, Cody back-tracked to the school, while Jade made her way to the back of the ambulance, doing her best to keep her balance. Although she had doubts about the plan, the idea of pushing open the door and calling for the dogs seemed easy enough, she thought, but a gut-instinct warned her of unseen obstacles. Sure enough, she was forced to stop dead in her tracks when suddenly, she found herself standing face-to-face with three terrified cats. Startled by Jade's approach, Sassy, ducked fast in the corner, and hid between Buddy and Buster. The three of them had enough excitement for one day, and were more than ready to get back home. In return, Jade was just a startled by the cats, as she stood staring in utter shock. "Cody, we seem to have a little problem back here." "Why? What's wrong?" he asked, hollering from the front. Keeping her eye on the cats, Jade was careful not to make any sudden movements... The last thing she wanted, was to spook the panicked trio into a state of hysteria. "Um, Cody, how do you feel about cats?" she asked. Puzzled by his classmate's seemingly, random question, Cody pressed for an answer. "Jade, what in the world are you talking about? What do you mean by cats?" he asked. "Cody, you know, cats, as in, meow-meow, whiskers and pointy ears." "Quit it with the riddles, Jade. Why are you bringing up cats, now?" he asked, keeping to his driving. Meanwhile, Jade was nervously, staring down at three, skittish felines, who looked ready to pounce. "Do I have to spell it out for you, Cody? C.A.T.S. THERE ARE THREE CATS BACK HERE AND THEY DON'T LOOK VERY HAPPY!" she said, raising her tone. "Well, geez, why didn't you just say so?" he hollered from the front. "I did say so!" "Well, how did they get back there?" "How should I know, Cody. If you want to know so bad, why don't you come back here and ask them yourself?" And with that, Cody instinctively slammed on the break. The abrupt stop sent Jade, and the trio of cats, tumbling clear across the rear of the ambulance, until landing hard against the back of Cody's seat. Jade instantly, found herself lying flat on her back, looking up at three, fuzzed-out cats, piled on top of her, all wearing a frenzied look of fear.

Everything happened fast following Jade's tumble with the cats. One minute, she found herself trapped beneath three, terrified balls of fur with claws, and in the next, she was shooing the spooked felines aside, and making her way to the ambulance rear door. Dealing with the mystery cats would have to wait, she thought, as her top priority was to find the missing dogs. It was a race against time, with the dog-catcher on the prowl. Acting fast, Jade pushed the door open, and began to call for Lilly. There, before her, mayhem plagued the school grounds. Filled with despair, she began to think she'd never find Lilly, or her friends. Meanwhile, Sassy dared herself to peek just beyond the open door, but alas, there was not a single dog in sight, and she too, secretly began to lose all hope.

Meanwhile, Buster began to feel the effects of his turbulent ride across town. "Is it just me, or does anyone else feel like throwing up?" he asked with a groan. His stomach was doing backflips, but Sassy took no pity on her nauseated brother. "Quit complaining, Buster and keep an eye out for the dogs!" she demanded. "Sassy, I feel so sick and just wanna go home. And besides, we'll never find the dogs in that mess." he said, looking to the crowd. Sassy hated to admit it, but her brother was probably right. So, hiding behind a self-assured facade, she continued to bark out orders. "Buster, you and Buddy, keep your eyes peeled. We're not leaving until the dogs are found!" Meanwhile, Jade continued to scope the crowd, but she too, was losing hope, and feared that Lilly was lost forever. Things continued to spiral out of control, and the cats regretted their decision to take a nap inside the ambulance. It was bad enough to wake up to Brian's fast drive across town, but they never imagined a fifth-grader to jump behind the wheel, and continue the terrorizing ride through the city. And so, as they sat trapped inside the ambulance, all they could do, was hope the dogs would be found, and everyone could just get home.

As time went by, Buster's nausea became more than he could handle. Sitting close by, Buddy noticed him turning unpleasant shades of green, and began to feel a little sick himself. But, Sassy continued to hide behind her self-assured front. "Suck it up, you two. We'll be out of this mess in no-time. The way I see it, once the girl manages to pull the dogs inside, the boy will probably just drive us all home." "Sassy, the last thing we need, is another fast ride in this stomach-turning, nausea-maker." Buster said. But little did he know, the ambulance ride would seem a piece of cake, compared to what was about to happen next...

A wave of panic flooded the schoolyard, as the hysterical crowd, fast became the perfect picture of chaos and confusion. Looking across the mob, Jade doubted she'd ever find the dogs. Kneeling at the back of the ambulance, she called to them once more, willing her voice to be heard. Meanwhile, Cody remained at the front, panning the area for the approaching police. The idling ambulance wouldn't be hard to miss, he thought. So, he pushed for Jade to hurry. "Speed it up back there, Jade. What's taking so long?" he asked, hollering from the driver's seat. Feeling the pressure, Jade didn't need reminders to work fast. "Cody, I'm doing the best I can, but if you think you can do better, then be my guest!" she hollered back. "Whatever, Jade. Just call the dogs!" he said. "I am, calling the dogs! What do you think I'm doing back here, knitting sweaters?" "Okay! Calm down. Just hurry!" "Cody, I'm doing the best I can, but there's a mob out here, and the dogs aren't anywhere in sight!" Filled with despair, Jade continued to cry out Lilly's name. Her trembling voice carried the sound of desperation, as it seemed unlikely, any of the dogs would hear her hollers over the commotion. Alas, just as she feared, the sound of her voice was lost in the uproar. Refusing to relent, she shouted Lilly's name again, and again, until her words penetrated the wall of noise, and her calls were finally heard.

Then, somewhere in the distance, surrounded by the crowd, Lilly's ears perked to the faint sound of Jade's voice. The little dog lifted her nose in an attempt to smell what she could only hear. *Could that be Jade?* she wondered. Listening, Lilly quickly realized that Jade must be close by. Harnessed in her wheel-cart, she worked her way through the crowd, pulling herself through a forest of legs, as she followed the sound of the young girl's voice, a familiar lullaby to her ear. "Jade, I'm here!" she called from afar, desperately trying to be heard. Alas, her anguished pleas, pierced the chaos and noise, and finally, caught Jade's ear. Turning to listen, she heard the distant barking, soon realizing, Lilly was nearby. Meanwhile, the wheel-chair bound dog continued to pull herself along, determined to find her friend. Her trembling limbs strained beneath the weight her load, as pure exhaustion took hold. Finally, emerging from the crowd, she spotted Jade, kneeling at the back of the ambulance. Her reactionary bark caught the young girl's ear, leading her to turn, and notice Lilly standing there before her. Their tear-filled eyes met in a moment of utter joy. It was then, Jade jumped from the ambulance just as Lilly dashed from the mob, and into the arms of the girl who promised to love her forever. There, they remained embraced, mirroring one another's thoughts... *I finally found her...*

Wrought with emotion, Jade pulled Lilly close. "I'm so glad you came back." she cried. "I promise never to leave you again." Her quivering chin segued to streams of tears, leaking from the corners of her eyes, until finally, relenting to an overpowering, raw emotion. Concerned by Jade's sadness, Lilly offered soft licks to her cheek, bringing a smile to her face, despite her glistening eyes. "Jade, it's okay. I'm with you now." Lilly said. Her words of comfort carried the sound of barking to the human ear. With that, Jade's face, beamed with happiness and shined through her teary eyes. Inspired by the dog she'd come to love, she began to recognize an inner magic that once lay dormant, and no longer would she hold herself hostage behind walls of fear and discontent.

Sitting there with Lilly by her side, she silently celebrated her new-found confidence, believing that anything was possible. And so, moments earlier when Jade spied Lilly emerging from the crowd, not only did she find the missing dog, but in essence, she discovered a piece of herself she once thought was gone forever...

Their tender moment came screeching to a halt at the sound of Cody's voice. "Come on, Jade. We need to get out of here!" he said, hollering from the driver's seat. Hearing the sirens, he knew the cops were hot on their trail. Backtracking to the school was a risky move, he thought, but it was their only choice, the dogs needed them. The stowaway cats were an added surprise, but Cody was in it for the long haul, and vowed to help them too. So, while Jade continued to call for the other dogs, he sat behind the wheel, scoping the area for the approaching police. Sure enough, he caught a glimpse of the blue lights in his side-view mirror. He knew they were cutting it close and needed to hightail it out of there fast. Just when he thought things were bad enough, the wailing siren of the tiller-truck caught his ear, and he knew it wouldn't be long before the area was swarming with police and firemen. "Jade, we need to hustle!" he hollered, in a voice drenched with panic. Feeling the pressure, Jade knew he was right, but she couldn't leave without the remaining dogs. With Lilly by her side, she scanned the area one last time. All seemed hopeless until suddenly, Champ sprang from the boisterous crowd, catching them both by surprise. His powerful howl easily penetrated the pre-existing noise. Filled with renewed hope, Jade figured, if Champ was nearby, then maybe the other dogs were too. Refusing to give up, she called across the noisy schoolyard one last time, but alas, the softness of her voice, was swallowed by the commotion. Her sinking heart dropped fathoms, at the mere thought of leaving without Lilly's friends. Making matters worse, Champ took off running, and once again, disappeared into the crowd. Down to the wire, Jade knew they had to get out of there fast. Without much choice, she turned to climb back inside the ambulance, until something caught her eye. Lilly also, reacted to the unexpected sight. Her bark was bold and fast. Much to Jade's relief, Oliver bolted from the crowd with Tino riding him like a galloping stallion. In a flash, the two spooked dogs, leapt into the back of the waiting ambulance. Pierre came next, running from the crowd. Acting fast, Jade lifted the panicked pooch inside the ambulance to join Oliver and Tino. There was no time to lose. She scanned the area for Clyde and Gizzy. Much to her relief, she spotted the two shih-tzu pulling from the mob. Clyde was in the lead, and Gizzy, a few paces behind. Running with all their might, they made their way to the waiting ambulance. Clyde wasn't about to get left behind, and Gaga, desperately wanted to get back to Edgar. Jade saw her opportunity, and swiftly, lifted them both inside to safety. Without a moment to spare, Lilly was pulled inside too, wheel-cart in all. "Mission accomplished!" Jade hollered to the front, as she pulled the door closed. Cody took his que. Eager to leave the scene, the determined young boy hit the gas, and the ambulance sped out of sight.

21 End of the Road

C ODY KEPT A VIGILANT EYE on the road, high on his mission to save the animals. Despite his young age, he maneuvered every turn, like a seasoned driver. It was plain to see, he was enjoying every minute of his thrill-ride across town. Conversely, Jade was a bundle of nerves. She held on tight with every hard turn he made. "Cody, this isn't one of your racing video games, you know!" "Yeah, I know, but it's still fun." he said, staring ahead. Giving him a look, Jade didn't appreciate his carefree attitude. "Cody, how can you say this is fun? We're running from the police in a stolen ambulance. That's not my idea of a good time. Just pull over and let me handle the driving." "No, Jade. I got it." "Cody, I'm older and taller." "Nice try, but I can handle it." he said. "You're way too young to be driving!" she shouted. "So are you, Jade!" he hollered back. Jade was fuming mad, and wasn't about to take no, for an answer. "I mean it, Cody! Pull this thing over, now!" she said, grabbing his arm. "Let go of me. I can handle this." he said, pushing her hand away. "Cody, you won't win this one. Now, stop the ambulance!" Suddenly, catching them both by surprise, they spotted blue lights from a fast-approaching police cruiser. Determined to get away, Cody hit the gas. "Catch me if you can!" he hollered, keeping a fierce eye on the road. "Cody, I think we'd better stop." Jade said, looking worried. "Jade, will you just relax? I have everything under control." he said, feeling confident. "And besides, we just saved a bunch of dogs. I'm sure the police will eventually, thank us." "I doubt it, Cody! The cops are chasing us because we took off in a city ambulance. Don't you see? They think we're thieves!" she said, feeling frustrated. "All right, just calm down, and take a deep breath. Like I told you before, once we get the animals to safety, we'll explain everything to the police. I wouldn't be surprised if Mayor Pearl held a parade in our honor." Jade shook her head. "Cody, you're living in a dream world. You do realize that, right?" "Think whatever you want, Jade. All I'm saying is, the hardest part is over. You'll see. I promise." With that, Jade sat there without another word, knowing at the end of the day, they'd have lots of explaining to do.

Before long, they found themselves stuck in crawling traffic. The police were trailing closely behind them, making a clean getaway seem impossible. Neither, Jade, nor Cody, typically broke rules, but a strong desire to save the dogs, pushed them to extremes. "Cody, we'll never get away with this." Jade said, looking ahead at the cars in front of them. He hated to admit it, but Jade might be right. And so, he thought hard to find a way to distance themselves from the police. Dawning on him, a flick of a switch would do the trick, he thought, as he reached for the control-panel. Lifting a lever, he brought the ambulance, screaming to life. Its ear-piercing siren, and flashing lights, signaled an emergency, thus causing the cluster of cars before them, to clear the way. "We're home-free now, Jade!" he shouted. Despite her apprehension, Jade couldn't resist a smile, as she braced herself for a wild ride. With the open road before them, Cody hit the gas and pushed the limits. Fearless and free, he drove at top speeds. "Hold on, Jade!" he hollered, as the ambulance sped out of town...

* * * *

It was a tight squeeze inside the ambulance. Feeling hungry and tired, the dogs and cats filled the cramped quarters. More than ever, all they wanted, was to be home in their safe and familiar surroundings. Sitting there, Lilly overheard the kids up front, planning a strategy to ensure everybody's safe return home. They were such brave, children to have taken on such a colossal mission, she thought. Looking around at the exhausted group, Lilly smiled to herself, as it warmed her heart, knowing her family went to such great lengths to bring her home. Their selfless act was a true testament of their genuine love, loyalty and bravery. Despite their valiant efforts, Lilly realized they were in a world of trouble for leaving the yard. So much was running through her tired mind at that moment. Thinking of Champ, she assumed he ran back to reunite with his handler. After all, his devotion and loyalty to Corey was like no other, and Lilly knew, they were the perfect crime fighting team.

Getting Gizzy back to her human was going to be another matter. Lilly assumed, old Edgar must be worried sick over his lost pet, and there was no doubt, Heidi was having a meltdown over her own missing dogs and cats. The worrisome possibilities began to cross her mind, as the tiring effects of being on the run, took a toll. Lilly fought to keep her sleepy eyes open, as pure exhaustion, enveloped every inch of her fatigued body. Strapped in her wheel-cart, she lay with her chest against the floor, longing for the comforts of her own, soft bed. Looking to the others through weary eyes, she could see that they too, were feeling the draining effects of their adventurous day. Smiling to herself, she thought of Tino, and the way he rode out the day, sitting on Oliver's back. Both such brave dogs, she thought, as she recalled the morning's events. Looking to Clyde and Gizzy, the two shih-tzu lay sprawled, side by side, seemingly without a care in the world, as they surrendered to their need for sleep. Meanwhile, Sassy sat alone, flat-eared, and furious, for if it weren't for the dogs, she thought, she'd never be in this mess to begin with. Buddy and Buster thought the same of Sassy, as it was her idea to follow the dogs. Finally, Pierre succumbed to his need for rest, as the gentle, old poodle lay with his face pressed against the floor, fast asleep. Their adventure-filled day was far from over, as Cody had another wild idea in mind, sure to keep everyone on the edge of their seats...

* * * *

Meanwhile, Corey drove at top speeds across town. With a tight grip on the wheel, and a heavy foot on the gas, he was determined to catch up to the runaway ambulance. He had just received word that Champ was found back at the school, and for that, he breathed a great sigh of relief. Oh, how he loved the oversized hound, as Champ was more than just a committed crime fighting partner, he was also, Corey's four-legged, best friend, and the very thought of losing him, tore at his heart. Then focusing on his mission, Corey knew, it was his duty to apprehend the thief who drove away in the ambulance. It never occurred to him that a child was at the controls, and was teaming up with another fifth grader, both on a daring mission to save the animals. Judging by the direction in which the ambulance was heading, Corey assumed, the driver would likely find themselves trapped on Baxter field with no place to run. He'd soon discover, he assumed wrong...

Jade braced herself for a dangerous ride, as Cody drove at top speeds, full of glory. Gripping the wheel, the fearless, young boy was determined to beat the odds. Sitting alongside him, Jade had no choice, but to put her trust in his skills, hoping his years of playing racing video games taught him something about real-life driving. She then thought of the dogs and cats riding in the back, and assumed they must be scared out of their minds. Agreeing to Cody's plan, she knew there'd be risks, but the situation was blowing out of control. And making matters worse, a quick glance out her side-view mirror, revealed beacons of blue from the approaching cruiser hot on their trail. "Cody, the cops are catching up to us!" she said, in a voice riddled with panic. She wasn't telling him anything he didn't already know. "Don't worry about a thing, Jade. I have everything under control." he said, pulling off the road and onto Baxter field. "What are you doing, Cody? Now we'll never get away!" she said, noticing the bumpy terrain. "Jade, I hope you're not afraid of heights." he said, driving full force across the field. Something in the distance caught Cody's eye, sure to be their ticket to freedom, he thought. The sky was the limit, literally...

22 *The Balloon*

A MOUNTAINOUS SILHOUETTE TOWERED OVER the field. Silently, it beckoned as a soft wind blew across the land. Splashes of yellow, filled the space as overgrown dandelions bowed their heads before the gentle giant. Prepared for a wingless flight, its fiery breath will soon lift it past a sea of clouds, where it will noiselessly float across an open sky, sure to decorate the heavens with its graceful presence. Adorned in splashes of blue and gold, it is the epitome of beauty and freedom. It is, a hot-air balloon…

Cody pulled from the road, and onto the field. As he maneuvered the ambulance across the hilly plain, the balloon was in his sights, only a few yards away. It was their only way out of there, he thought, as he envisioned a ride, a mile in the sky. Meanwhile, Jade did her best to keep to her seat, as the ambulance continued its turbulent tour across the wide-open space. "Cody, I'm not so sure this is such a good idea." she said, her voice sounding choppy, as they hit every bump. "So, you don't think we should take the balloon?" he asked, focusing ahead. "Well, I think it's a little extreme, don't you?" she asked. "Oh, come on, Jade. We went way past extreme when we took the ambulance." "I realize that Cody, but you don't know the first thing about ballooning." "Technically, that's true, but I mean, how hard can it be?" he said, feeling sure of himself. With that, Jade rolled her eyes. "Cody, you realize, we have an ambulance full of dogs and cats, right? I don't know how you expect us to load them onto the balloon. Just face it, we're doomed." "Jade, just relax. Trust me, I know what I'm doing. Besides, imagine the story this will make for your grandchildren someday." "Grandchildren? That'd be the day. I'll be lucky enough to make it to adulthood if I keep hanging around with you." And with that, they continued their bumpy drive across the field, and prepared for the next phase of their daring mission to save the animals.

* * * *

Sitting in the cruiser, Corey watched the ambulance from distance. A recent phone call from Mister Alan, alerted him that Jade and Cody were the ones behind the mind-blowing police chase. Backing off, he didn't want to scare them any more than they probably already were. Looking through his binoculars, it was easy to see the ambulance moving across Baxter field. With only one entry point, the kids would eventually find themselves trapped, with nowhere to run, he thought. Little did he know, Cody had other ideas, sure to leave the police and fire department, scrambling to stop them.

* * * *

The increasing winds, tugged at the ropes, anchoring the majestic craft. A grand and spectacular sight, the balloon stood tall above the ground, swaying gracefully in the breeze. Blasts of fiery, hot air, poured from the burner, and into the nylon belly, as it prepared to journey, deep into the cloudless sky. Destined to carry a precious cargo on an ocean of air, the gondola will remain adrift, high above the earthy plain. Wisps of painted clouds, adorning the nylon body, create a gentle camouflage against the pre-summer sky. Jade and Cody, marveled at the breathtaking sight, knowing that in just a moment's time, they too, will be one with the clouds.

23 *On the Run*

T HE BALLOON STOOD ONLY YARDS away but felt like miles to the kids running against the wind. Pumping their legs with all their might, it was a race to the gondola before the cops caught up to them. Cody spotted the cruiser and tiller-truck, parked at a distance, and knew, they had to move fast. "Jade, keep running!" he shouted, sprinting towards the balloon. "Cody, we'll never make it!" she hollered back. "Don't talk, Jade. Just keep running!" "Cody, I am, running!" she said, as burning breaths caught in her throat. Cody wasn't far ahead. A quick glance over his shoulder, revealed the dogs and cats trailing closely behind. Harnessed in her wheel-cart, Lilly pulled herself along. Brave and determined, the wheelchair-bound dog, dug her claws, deep into the ground, and moved across the land with incredible speed. Tino was seen next, racing across the bumpy terrain, riding Oliver like a hurdle-jumping horse. Pierre ran along, pumping his short legs, tripping and stumbling along the way, as he pushed through tall blades of crabgrass, slapping at his face. Clyde and Gizzy weren't far behind. Matching strides, the two shih-tzu ran through dandelion patches, as splashes of yellow, filled the land as far as the eye could see. Meanwhile, the cats took on a more tactile approach, racing across the open plain. Sassy crept low over the ground, looking skittish and edgy. Buddy and Buster did the same, trailing the group, dreading their fearful, ride in the sky.

* * * *

Finally, all were gathered before the majestic craft. While the kids marveled at its enormity, the dogs and cats dared themselves to approach, as they too, seemed to be gauging its colossal size. Dwarfed by the balloon, Cody ran his eyes from the base of the gondola, all the way up to the top of its nylon belly. Stunned by its towering height, he stood wide-eyed, in amazement, knowing that in a moment's time, he'll be aboard the monstrous airship, floating high above Baxter field. Meanwhile, Jade had been circling the gondola, looking for a way to climb aboard. They were cutting it close with the police and fireman fast approaching. "If we're gonna do this, Cody, we need to do it, now!" she said, noticing the men. "Yeah, I guess we should get moving." he said, unsure of how to proceed. "You guess? Cody, what's that's supposed to mean? Don't even tell me you're changing your mind about this." "No, of course not." he said, but Jade sensed the reality of what they were about to do, was hitting him hard. "Cody are you sure you're still up for this?" she asked, giving him an out. "Absolutely! Flying this thing will be is a piece of cake." he said, trying to sound convincing. "Whatever you say, Cody. Keep telling yourself that, and maybe you'll actually believe it." she said, giving him a look. "I'm serious, Jade. I got this. You'll see." "If you say so, Cody, but we have to go, now!" she said, feeling the pressure. Looking across the way, she noticed the police and fire department, fast approaching. To her surprise, the gym-teacher and guidance counselor were heading their way too. Brenden and Jeremy weren't about to miss any of the action. Although it was their job to foster self-confidence in all their students, taking off in a hot-air balloon, was not what they had in mind. Jeremy marveled at the way Jade and Cody took on such a harrowing mission to save the animals. It was then, his thoughts trailed back to his own children, Marlee and Charlie. Smiling to himself, he thought of Marlee's level of confidence, and Charlie's eagerness to keep up with his big sister, and knew, when it came to his children, anything was possible. Meanwhile, Brenden continued his run across the field. Determined to stop the kids, there was a part of him that admired them for their bravery, and bold attempt to fight for what they believed in. Their fearless actions were nothing short of remarkable, but despite that, the race to the gondola continued. Corey, Jeremy, Brenden, Elliot and Brian, ran at top speeds, doing their best to catch up to the runaway kids. In some unique way, they appreciated what Jade and

Cody, were trying to accomplish, knowing the kids believed that the dogs and cats were in great peril. It was a selfless act, despite the dangers they faced. Their courage and bravery were evident in every bold action they'd taken, and for that, they were commended. But at the end of the day, they were mere children, who dared themselves to take on the world, without realizing, that putting themselves in harm's way, wasn't the answer.

* * * *

Cody worked fast to release the sandbags anchoring the balloon. Meanwhile, Jade began the task of loading the dogs and cats inside the gondola. They were cutting close, as the men were fast approaching. They needed a swift lift-off, but as bad luck would have it, the balloon sat like lead in the middle of the field. "Cody, why are we still grounded?" Jade asked, looking worried. The load of animals must be too much for the balloon to lift, she thought. "Jade, hold on a minute." he said, working fast. "But we don't have a minute! We have to go, now!" The police officer was ascending upon them. "Give me a second. I'm pretty sure I just figured it out." he said, working the controls. They were down to only seconds. "We'll never make it, Cody!" she said, noticing Corey running towards them. Determined to stop the kids, he made his fast approach. Standing in the gondola, Jade's eyes locked with his. She was ready for battle. It was game-on, she thought, determined to save the animals. A whirlwind of thoughts swirled through her mind. In a moment of regret, she felt sorry, and afraid, but in the end, it was Lilly and her friends who mattered most. With that final thought, the balloon began to rise. Jade remained locked in Corey's stare, as he jumped for the balloon. "Catch me if you can." she said, with a smirk, as the gondola lifted from the ground. Standing beside her, Cody lifted his arms in victory. "We did it, Jade!" he shouted. And with that, the grand airship gained altitude, and soared across the sky.

24 Up and Away...

THE BALLOON CONTINUED ITS GREAT ascent, carrying the gondola and its precious cargo, high above the field. The men watched in disbelief, as the spectacular craft escaped their reach, rising to greater heights. Jade and Cody took their ride, while the panicked group scurried below. The faint sound of their distant voices began to fade, as the balloon climbed higher in the sky. Powerful blasts of air traded places with the previous softer winds, carrying the gondola across an ocean of air. Standing side by side, the children silently celebrated their victorious moment, as they took in the grand and spectacular view. Captivated by its allure, Jade looked to the horizon as mighty wind gusts blew past her petite frame, pulling hard at her hair. Cody, also felt the slapping gale whip across his chest, causing his nylon jacket to flap uncontrollably in the strong air current. Ready for adventure, he was in his element, as he stood alongside Jade, and looked across the great beyond. Both indulging in private thoughts, feeling free, and teetering on the threshold of fear, yet welcoming the thrill-ride that would trump all rides..

* * * *

Rising high above the earthy plain, the air grew cool, as the majestic craft noiselessly, floated past a layer of stratus clouds. Jade leaned into the breeze; the crisp air heightened her senses and washed away the fears that for too long, anchored her lively spirit. Drawing in deep breaths, she welcomed the biting air that filled her lungs, while a swoosh of wind, blew past her ears. Cody looked to her, as she stood quietly, focusing her gaze across the heavens... He wondered what thoughts might be flooding her worried mind. "Jade are you afraid?" he asked. The increasing gale, pulled hard, causing his voice to pale in comparison to the noisy gusts. Facing the open sky, Jade stood staring ahead, as a rush air blew past her face, and streamed through the silky strands of her ebony locks. Maintaining her gaze, the balloon lifted them higher across a blissful paradise. Finally, answering his question, Jade spoke softly... "For the first time in my life, I forgot to be afraid." she said. And with that, she bravely, prepared to combat the forces of nature, as the gondola drifted across a boundless and darkening sky...

25 All Hands on Deck

I T WAS A TIGHT SQUEEZE inside the gondola. Lilly sat curled alongside the other dogs and cats. The break from her wheel-cart was a welcomed relief, as her muscles felt tied up in knots. Meanwhile, the balloon gained altitude, causing the once tepid air to grow cool and damp, adding to her achy feel. Pangs of hunger pulled hard, as did her need for sleep, but food and rest would come later, she thought. Looking to the others, the cats seemed surprisingly calm, despite their unsettling ride, but Lilly knew it wouldn't be long before they too, balked at their unforgiving flight across a stormy sky. Conversely, the dogs sensed the impending danger... The gondola continued its ascent, deeper into the great infinity, as powerful wind gusts, shook it with cyclone force. The gentle sway of their once peaceful glide, suddenly changed to a turbulent excursion one thousand feet above a raging sea. Full of fear, the animals sat huddled, as the balloon soared across the threatening sky at the mercy of nature's wrath. Meanwhile, Jade and Cody prepared to face their toughest challenge of all, as shifting air currents added to their convulsive flight. Scattered raindrops began to tap against the giant craft; a prelude of worst to come. Whistling winds, eerily sang their song, and the kids soon realized, the weather was drastically changing for the worst. Remaining vigilant, they vowed to protect the animals, who huddled by their feet. And so, keeping an eye on the horizon, Cody spotted the menacing force up ahead. "Thunderheads at twelve o'clock!" he shouted, cupping his hands at the sides of his mouth. Standing alongside him, Jade could do without his theatrics. "Cody, you don't have to yell. I'm standing right next to you." she said, rolling her eyes. "Well, you better brace yourself, Jade, because we're headed straight for a storm!" he said, pointing towards a blackened mountain of clouds, blocking their path. Noticing the monstrous billow, Jade knew they were in big trouble. "Cody, we have to turn around!" The raging cyclone was about to rip them to shreds. "Jade, I hate to be the bearer of bad news, but we're at the mercy of this storm. We can't just turn around." "So, what can we do?" she asked, wearing a look of fear. "Jade, the only thing we can do, is hope the balloon isn't shredded like paper in the wind." "Cody, you can't be serious!" "Jade, listen to me. We'll get through this one way or another. I promise." "Yeah, well, in the future, remind me never to listen to you again." she said, giving him a look. And with that, the kids prepared to battle the powerful forces of nature. Giving it their all, Jade and Cody, refused to go down without a fight...

26 Sending Out an SOS

"**WHAT DO YOU MEAN THE** kids got away?" Pacing back and forth in his office, Mister Alan demanded answers. It was his responsibility to ensure the safety of his students, and maintain the integrity of the school. How two fifth graders managed to flee in a hot-air balloon, was beyond him. Meanwhile, Corey stood by the door, while Jeremy and Brenden, sat in front of the desk. All wearing the same look of dread, the weight of the world, rested on their shoulders, as they believed, it was their responsibility to bring Jade and Cody home. "Look, were doing the best we can. We'll get the kids back." Corey said, trying to sound reassuring. Brenden shot him a look. "Quit it with the, *everything will be just fine,* garbage. You know, just as well as we do, things don't look good, Corey!" "Hey, I'm not about to give up on those kids and neither should you, Brenden." "Who said anything about giving up?" "Well, just listen to yourself." Corey said, snapping back.

Brenden's eyes grew wild with fury, and his powerful voice, pounded off the walls, as he shouted across the small office space. "Listen, Corey. I'm not giving up! I'm just being realistic!" Meanwhile, Jeremy noticed things getting heated, and stepped in between the arguing men. "Knock it off, you two. We're not helping Jade or Cody, by fighting about this." he said. Brenden rolled his eyes. "Oh, here we go again. The guidance counselor saves the day, with his psychology degree." "Look, Brenden. I'm not trying to save anybody's day. All I'm saying is, we should be focusing on getting the kids back, not going at each other's throats." Corey nodded in agreement. "Jeremy has a point. Besides, we have a lot of eyes looking for them, as we speak. So, let's just keep positive about this." he said. Meanwhile, Mister Alan kept quiet, hoping that Corey was right. As if on que, an authoritative rap at the door caught everyone's attention. Elliot and Brian stood at the threshold. Their grim expressions spoke volumes, as they prepared to deliver unsettling news. "Gentlemen, please come inside and take a seat." Mister Alan said, motioning with his hand. Stepping into the office, the squawk from their radios, echoed throughout the space, and spilled into the corridor. All eyes were on them, as Elliot prepared to provide an update. "We had no choice, but to involve the Coast Guard. They dispatched an emergency response team. The balloon-craft was pulled offshore by high intensity winds. They have a visual, but without a doubt, the kids are in extreme danger."

* * * *

Torrential rain pelted the balloon, cooling the air inside the nylon belly, causing the weakening craft to plunge from the sky. Raging winds pulled it towards a fleet of storm clouds hanging low over the horizon like a wall of impenetrable darkness. The thunderheads loomed before them. A formidable opponent indeed, Cody thought, as he welcomed the challenge to do battle with such a menacing force. Conversely, Jade looked towards the hungry sky, and feared the wrath of nature's temper tantrum, as sheets of rain poured from the heavens like waterfalls in the sky. Chilled to the bone, with no place to take cover, they shivered beneath the onslaught of the stormy sky. Jade wrapped her arms around herself, as her shivering body trembled with cold. "I'm freezing, Cody." "I know, Jade, but try to hang in there." he said. "Cody, this is hopeless. Just look at us! Were both soaking wet, and we're about to crash in the middle of the Boston harbor!" "Listen to me, Jade. I won't let that happen. All I need to do, is keep enough hot air inside the balloon, and we'll be home-free." "Sure, Cody. Like I haven't heard that before." "Just relax, Jade. Together, we can do this." he said, trying to calm her. With that, Jade's expression went from worried, to wicked. "Cody, stop telling me to relax! Do I need to remind you of our current situation? And not only that, but the dogs and cats are scared to death!" "All right, already. I get it, Jade. But what did you want me to say? That we'll probably never see the likes of tomorrow?" At the sound of his own words, Cody silently began to fear the worst...

The elements fast became too much to bear, as the kids worked to shield the animals from the wind-swept rain, an impossible feat under the thunderous sky. Drifting further offshore, their peaceful glide above Baxter field, morphed into a turbulent ride, suspended over the harbor. Looking down upon the briny deep, a crash-landing seemed imminent. Blasts of stormy air blew hard across the water's surface, creating monstrous swells. Wracked with fear, the kids clung to the gondola, as swirling rushes of air pushed and pulled at the craft, shaking them without mercy.

* * * *

The animals huddled inside the cramped gondola, a far cry from the warmth and safety of their home. Shivering with cold, they bravely endured their topsy turvy ride, trying in vain to shield themselves from the biting winds, tearing across the blackened sky. A howling gale created an eerie feel, as ghostly calls beckoned from the heavens. Lilly lay curled, full of regret. Learning a hard lesson, she vowed, never again to seek adventure beyond the realms of her own backyard. After all, riding out an angry storm across an untamed sky, was not exactly what she'd bargained for, when she planned her trip to school. Surely, the other dogs felt the same, she thought. And there was no doubt, Sassy didn't appreciate the drenching effects of the wind-swept rain, as her once fluffy coat, lay flat against her shivering body. Buddy and Buster faired no better, as they too, sat soaked, flat-eared and chilled to the bone. Why they ever agreed to journey from their sunny windowsill was beyond them. And so, there they were, sitting alongside the dogs, at the mercy of the wind. Lilly looked around at the exhausted group. It was easy to see, the day's events took a tiring toll. Surely, Gizzy was eager to get home to her person, and no doubt, Clyde was craving a snack. All Pierre desired, was to curl in the comforts of his own warm bed. Meanwhile, old Tino buried his face in Oliver's back, a futile attempt to hide from the stinging rain. Sitting there, Lilly marveled at the way her family took on the day with such aplomb... All remained quiet, as everyone braced for the next violent wind-gust. It was then, Lilly turned an ear to the faint sound of Buster's voice... "One, two, three..." he began. "Four, five, six..." she heard again. "Buster why are you counting?" she asked, looking puzzled. "Lilly, the better question is, what am I counting?" he said. "Okay then, Buster. Tell me, what is it that you're counting?" she asked, playing along. "Funny you should ask." he began. "What I'm merely trying to do, is calculate the number of lives I have left." "Buster, what in the world, are you talking about?" Lilly asked, feeling annoyed. Buster was quick to reply. "Lilly, everybody knows, a cat has nine lives." Nodding her head, Lilly was beginning to understand. "Buster, I hate to be the bearer of bad news, but that's just a myth. Cats get only one life, just like dogs. So, if I were you, I'd think twice before ever leaving the yard again." Listening nearby, Sassy didn't approve of Lilly's revelation. "Well, that's just great, Lilly." Sassy said, in a voice riddled with sarcasm. "Buster's

132

already scared enough as it is, and now, you have to go and tell him, he's got only one life, not nine!" "Oh, Sassy, lighten up. I don't see what the big deal is. Besides, he needed to know truth. I'm sure he'll forget all about it soon enough, because like most cats, he has a short attention span." Lilly reasoned. Sassy did not appreciate her sister's comment. "So, you think that cats have short attention spans, do you? Well, at least we cats aren't foolish enough to play games of fetch with our humans. Only a simple-minded dog would partake in such redundant act. The whole concept makes no sense to me." Sassy said, with her nose in the air. "But then again, what could I possibly know? I mean, after all, I'm just a cat with a short attention span, right?" she said, giving Lilly an angry look. And so, it was then, they put their differences aside, and hoped the gondola was strong enough to withstand a crash-landing...

* * * *

The helicopter traveled high above the shoreline. Gale-force winds were reaching speeds of forty knots, but still no match for the beating blades of the twin-engine Jayhawk; one of the Coast Guard's finest pieces of equipment, designed for search and rescue. Sitting at the controls, the guardsman's trained eye scanned the perimeter, determined to locate the lost balloon-craft, easily dwarfed by the mountainous ocean swells. Suddenly, noticing the wreckage about a mile offshore, he called in the coordinates, and a response boat team was dispatched.

* * * *

Rushes of stormy air shook the dangling gondola, as it hung inches above the ocean's surface. Cody did his best to keep the craft from plummeting into the icy water, but the drenching rains worked against him. If only he could keep enough hot air inside the nylon belly, then maybe they'd make it to the mainland, he thought. Caught in a swirling current, the gondola dipped and swayed over the rising sea. Jade looked down upon their precious cargo, huddled by her feet. The dogs and cats were shivering with cold, as frigid seawater, seeped inside, surrounding them in a salty puddle. "Cody, we'll never survive this! The poor animals are starting to panic!" Their situation seemed hopeless, she thought, as rolling ocean swells slapped at the dangling balloon like monstrous hands clawing from the sea. "Jade, listen to me. If we could just get past this downpour, then maybe we'll make it back to the mainland." he said, talking over the rain. "Cody, did you just say, *maybe*? What's that supposed to mean?" she asked, looking worried. "Oh c'mon, Jade. I didn't mean to say, maybe. Of course, we'll make it back to land." he said, trying to sound reassuring. Searching his eyes for an ounce of truth, she knew better than to believe him. "You don't seem so sure about that, Cody." "Look, I told you before, I won't let anything happen to either one of us, or the animals we vowed to protect." She wanted to believe him, but the rising sea was reaching the bottom of the gondola, and ocean swells, morphed into mountains all around them. They were hovering only inches above the water's vast and furious surface, and could feel the ocean's wrath pounding at their feet. Then, without warning, a savage green wave washed over the gondola, knocking them both backwards. Working to catch her breath, Jade angrily looked to her classmate, as she wiped the burning saltwater from her eyes. Why she ever agreed to the balloon ride in the first place, was beyond her. "Jade, are you all right?" Cody asked, helping her to her feet. "I'm all right, Cody, but you won't be when I'm done with you." she said, coughing up water. "Why? What did I do?" he asked. "Cody, this was all your idea. I should have never listened to you to begin with." Without a moment to reply, another monstrous wave hit with mighty force. Struggling to keep to their feet, the kids feared the worst, as the gondola skimmed across the surface of the great and unexplored. Wave after wave, the balloon took its beating, while Jade and Cody clung to the sides, doing their best to stay afloat. Gagging saltwater splashed at their face, thus stinging their eyes. Plagued with terror, Jade realized her unimaginable reality, as the gondola began to sink. They were destined to be one with the darkened depths of a cold, and remote ocean floor. The hungry ocean slowly bit at the sinking craft, like a liquid serpent, methodically swallowing its prey. The dogs and cats sat trapped inside the watery tomb, as the icy sea spilled inside, numbing their treading limbs. Frigid saltwater poured inside from all four sides, pulling the broken craft beneath the ocean's smothering surface. Jade looked hopelessly at the panicked faces around her. This can't be happening, she thought, as the gondola filled with bone-chilling water. Cody tried in vain to ignite the burner, but the drenching rain worked against him. Watching her classmate fight for the lives he vowed to protect, Jade knew there'd be no winning, and ultimately succumbed to their fate. It was, game-over, she thought. There were no second chances. It was do or die, and Jade feared the latter...

* * * *

Suddenly, submerged in a frigid sea, Jade's muffled screams of terror went unheard, as she fell deeper into the great abyss. Disoriented by a deep, dark sea, the way to the surface was lost in her blindness. But nature showed mercy on the panicked young girl, as lightning cracked the sky, illuminating the abysmal plane, thus guiding her path. Full of fear, Jade's swim to the surface felt like miles, as a searing burn, tore inside her chest. Holding her breath, she broke through the top, gasping for air, welcoming the life-saving oxygen filling her hungry lungs. Surrounded by darkness, she worked to stay afloat, treading water fathoms deep. Her dangling legs, kicked beneath the water's surface, sure to lure carnivorous predators from the blackened, watery world beneath her. Plagued with terror, she remained alone, crying for help in a bottomless sea. The salty brine showed no mercy, as the stinging waves ravished her skin and burned at her eyes. Then slipping beneath the smothering surface, the stormy ocean morphed into an unforgiving beast, savagely swallowing her whole. Filled with terror, Jade thrashed in the surf, trying in vain to free herself from the mouth of the watery giant. Barely keeping her chin above the surface, she searched for Cody, but it was impossible to see through the impenetrable darkness. Suddenly, a flash of lightning revealed Cody and the animals, clinging to the wreckage, fighting against the whipping winds, powerful enough to rip them from their only place of refuge. "Cody, save me! I'm sinking!" she called out, but the rain fell like stones against the water's surface, blocking her cries for help. Growing weaker by the second, the surging current pushed against her weary body. Jade was losing her fight against nature's wrath. Her only hope of survival, was to reach the fleeing wreckage, but with each strobe of lightning, she could see Cody and the animals, drifting further from her reach.

* * * *

The twin-engine chopper hovered above the stormy surf, as the rescue mission unfolded. Barely visible to the naked eye, the balloon-craft lay wrecked amid the rolling sea. But with thermal imaging technology, the lost could be found, and Cody was spotted in the distance, clinging to the dilapidated gondola. Suspended below the hovering helicopter, the life-saving basket, swayed in the wind, as the guardsman lowered it to collect his casualty. Cody reached for the basket, but his weakening grip was no match for the ferocious waves, slapping against the sinking craft. Plagued with cold, his body grew numb, as did his mind. The young boy was fading fast, and it was all he could do, to keep from sliding into the mouth of the hungry sea. The elements took a brutal toll, as he clung to life, amid nature's temper tantrum. Fighting against delirium, Cody's conscious mind began to retreat, while the bitter cold ravished his shivering body. Meanwhile, somewhere in the distant, drowning sea, Jade continued to call for help. Her beseeching cries from the smothering waves, caught his ear, but alas, Cody's reality grew dim, and he began to slip into a blissful, unconscious world.

Meanwhile, quivering with fear, the cats and dogs hopelessly clung to the sinking gondola. "Well, Sassy, this is a fine mess you've gotten us into!" Buster said, shouting over the howling winds. His rain-soaked fur, lay flat against his shivering body; the skittish cat was scared out of his mind. "Oh, no ya don't, Buster!" Sassy warned, waving her paw in his face. "Don't even think about pinning this one on me!" she began. "Buster, if you remember correctly, it was yours and Buddy's idea to take a nap inside the ambulance to begin with, and if I hadn't listened to you two, I wouldn't be fighting for my life in this oversized fishbowl! And allow me to point out the obvious here... We're stranded in the middle of the Atlantic Ocean, barely afloat on what's left of this broken-down gondola, and to make matters worse, we're about to become shark-bait!" Sassy was fuming. Meanwhile, Lilly knew the importance of keeping everybody calm, and wasn't about to let her family become a three-course meal for whatever might be lurking in the depths beneath them. "Just stop it, you two! If it's anybody's fault at all, it's mine." she said. Sassy shook her head. "Okay, Lilly. But even if we agree that we're in this mess all because of your need to explore beyond the confines of our backyard, it still doesn't change the fact, that we're drifting out to sea on a dilapidated pile of junk. And in case you haven't noticed, Cody is barely conscious. Not to mention, Jade is nowhere in sight, and is probably sitting in the belly of a gigantic blue-whale, by now." "Sassy, don't be ridiculous. I doubt she was swallowed by a man-eating beluga." Lilly said. "And besides, the Coast Guard just sent help. So, while you take turns, riding up to the chopper in the basket, I'll make a swim for it, and look for Jade." With that, Oliver tried to sway his sister from making a deadly mistake. "Lilly, you can't just expect to jump into the middle of the ocean and survive all this." he said, referring to the stormy swells. "Ollie, I don't have a choice. Jade needs me." she explained. "I understand that you want to help, but remember, you're at a slight disadvantage." Oliver said, referring to her disability. "Disadvantage?" Lilly asked, looking puzzled. Then dawning on her, she realized what Oliver was implying. "Oh, I see now. So, you assume that because I'm a wheelchair-bound dog, I must be helpless, right? Ollie, you should know by now, I'm far from incapable, and not afraid to jump into that oversized tide-pool to save the girl who needs me. I'll do whatever it takes to help her, even if it's the last thing I do, and I refuse to let a few, little waves, stand in my way!" Despite his best efforts, Oliver knew there'd be no winning with his sister. "Okay, Lilly, but please be careful." he said. "I appreciate your concern, Ollie, but don't worry, I got this." Lilly said, as she prepared for her marathon swim.

Meanwhile, just overhead, the Coast Guard's rescue team made their fast approach. Lilly's ears perked at the sound of the hovering helicopter. Then nudging the semi-conscious boy, she knew their help was vital. The rescue-basket hung just beyond Cody's reach. Lilly barked once more, trying to rouse him, but the sound of her voice was muffled by the howling winds. Huddled alongside them, the others fared no better. Clyde and Gizzy were barely hanging on to the wreckage. Their rain-soaked coats, lay pasted against their shivering bodies. Pierre trembled beneath his sopping curly fur, while Oliver did his best to shield Tino from the whipping winds. Despite the obvious dangers, it was the water, Sassy and the other cats feared most, but it would be the powerful gale-force that would rip them from their stronghold, and feed them to the ferocious sea.

Cody's vow to protect the animals was lost in his battle against the extreme forces of nature. Growing weaker by the second, he reached for the dangling basket, one last time, but it was no use, he was falling fast into an unconscious world. Clinging to the wreckage, Lilly barked once more, trying in vain to stop the inevitable, but the young boy could hold on, no longer, and slowly, slipped into the mouth of a behemoth wave... Suddenly, emerging from the mist, a fleet of lifeboats converged like a calvary at sea, and pulled Cody's limp and unconscious body to safety. The dogs and cats were next, as they too, sat inside the rubber rafts, and prepared for a fast drive back to the mainland. All but Jade, were accounted for. Sensing she wasn't far, Lilly turned her radar-like ears, and detected the faint sound of the lost girl's cries for help. "Jade, I'm coming to save you!" she shouted, but her calls of reassurance carried the sound of barking, to the human ear. Turning, the guardsmen looked to the yelping dog, and assumed her reaction was due to the storm, but it was Jade, who Lilly was calling for. Off in the distance, behind a wall of waves, he finally spotted the panicked girl, thrashing in the surf. Futile attempts to keep her chin above the surface, added to her terrifying swim, as gagging splashes of water, trickled down her throat. Refusing to sit idle, Lilly pushed herself from the life-raft, and into the raging surf. Paddling against the tide, she swam with all her might, in a desperate attempt to save her drowning friend.

Helpless against the surging sea, Jade's legs felt like lead, as the pulling current dragged her underwater. Fighting for air, her lungs felt ablaze, burning inside her chest. Stinging saltwater, tore at her eyes, as wave after wave, slapped at her face. Meanwhile, Lilly forged ahead, paddling across the hilly swells, rising and falling over the rolling sea. Jade caught a glimpse of the dog, off in the distance, heading in her direction. Fearful for Lilly's safety, Jade was sure a dog as small as she, would succumb to the swirly deep. Both of them fought against the surf, but alas, the forces of nature kept them apart. The winds continued to blast against the water's surface, creating swells as tall as mountains, but Lilly refused to succumb to nature's fury. Remaining steadfast, she pulled herself across a stormy sea. Jade did the same, refusing to relent to nature's bullying, but soon realized, nature was not limited to only wind and rain, for somewhere in the distance, she spotted a menacing dorsal fin slicing across the water's surface with incredible speed, and was heading in her direction. It could mean only one thing, Jade thought... Shark! Surrounded by mountainous swells, dark and deep, she had no place of refuge, and was helpless against the fierce force of nature, rapidly swimming towards her. It really was, game-over, she thought. Her limbs grew numb, as did her mind. And so, it was then, she'd concede to defeat against her battle with the elements. Her conscious mind began to fade as she began to transcend into a peaceful existence, and journey to place where danger ceased to exist, and bullying was a thing of the past. Drifting... she allowed herself to voyage to a place where kittens governed the land, and angelfish ruled the sea. Peacefully, closing her eyes one last time, Jade continued her journey to another place and time...

27 *The Bus Stops Here*

THE INTRUSIVE SOUND, JARRED HER from her sleepy world...
The incessant beeping, pulled hard, thus dragging her back to a state of consciousness. Jade awakened as if it were an emergency, until focusing her thoughts, while she lay entangled in the bed sheets. Her heart began to slow, as a restless and broken sleep, left her fatigued by a night filled with tossing and turning. Feeling exhausted despite her sleep, she could hardly believe it was time to wake up and start the day. Surely, the timekeeper was fooling her, but the clock didn't lie. However, in some strange way, she believed the inanimate object enjoyed rousing her from a much-needed rest. With her sleepy face buried in her pillow, she blindly reached for the alarm-clock and fumbled for the snooze button. Finally, putting a stop to the intrusive noise disturbing her sleep, she lay sprawled, catching her breath from the nocturnal escapade that kept her on the run. On this morning,

she welcomed the wake-up call. Reeling from her unsettling nightmare, she pulled back the sheets, thankful to be alive. She sleepily padded her way to the dresser, and stood before the mirror, barely recognizing her own reflection. Her disheveled looks matched the way she felt. Yawning, she turned to get dressed, as a familiar pit, gnawed at her gut. It wouldn't be long before she'd face the meanest girl in class, she thought. Falling from one nightmare, and into the next, she knew Rilee was a sizable opponent in a proverbial, shark infested world. Knowing well what horrors awaited, Jade faced the morning, full of dread. But despite her fear, she forged on, hoping that each day might offer the peace and safety, every child deserved to experience while at school. The bus would soon arrive, and she knew, there was no escaping the inevitable. Rilee, undoubtedly, would be at the bus-stop in true form, ruthless in nature, and unequivocally, the most unkind girl in her class. Although her presence was not without censure, nobody dared challenge the kid who'd rip you to shreds without provocation. So, accepting her fate, Jade finished getting dressed, just as her mother called from the kitchen. "Honey, hurry along now. The bus will be here any minute." she warned. "Okay, Mom. I'll be right there!" Jade said, calling from the bedroom. Feeling anxious, she pulled on her backpack, and started for the door... "Jade honey, before you go, sit down and eat something." her mother said, placing a plate on the table. "No thanks, Mom." "But I made your favorite. You never refuse banana pancakes." "I know, Mom, but I'm just not very hungry right now, that's all." "What's the matter, Jade?" You haven't been yourself in weeks." "I'm fine, Mom. I just need to get going, or I'll miss the bus." "Sweetheart, is everything okay at school? You can talk to me, you know." Pausing a moment, Jade was tempted to share the burden, but decided against risking her parents calling the principal. The embarrassment would be too much to bear, she thought, and surely, Rilee would accuse her of an inability to fight her own battles. Alas, she kept her secret, and assured her mother, that all was well. Glancing out the window, she caught a glimpse of the kids, congregating at the bus-stop, Jade knew then, it was time to go. After giving her mother a kiss on the cheek, she was out the door, to join the others across the street.

* * * *

Cody was first to spot her running up to the stop. "It's about time, Jade. I didn't think you were going to make it." "Yeah, I know. I sort of overslept." she said, slightly winded. "What do you mean, you *sort of* overslept?" he asked, looking puzzled. "Well, after last night's bad dream, I feel like I'm still half asleep." she said, looking less than bright-eyed. "Well, you'd better wake up fast, because Rilee is heading this way. Sure enough, the bully made her abrupt approach and pushed Jade to the ground. "Good morning, sleepyhead. What's the matter, having trouble waking up for school today?" The bully's tone was drenched with mockery. Caught off guard by the early morning assault, Jade remained stunned, sitting on the pavement, looking up at Rilee. Having just witnessed the bully's ambush, Cody stepped in, determined to protect his classmate. "Leave her alone, Rilee, or else I'm gonna..." he started to say, but Rilee cut him off mid-sentence. "Or else what, Cody? Do you honestly think, you have what it takes to stand up to me?" she asked. Cody knew Rilee had a point. After all, she was the meanest kid in school. Meanwhile, Jade appreciated his brave efforts, but what was going on between she and Rilee, didn't involve him, and she didn't want him getting hurt coming to her defense. "Leave Cody out of this, Rilee. This is between you and me." she dared herself to say. Surprised by Jade's bold attempt, Rilee decided to up her game, and implement her best intimidation tactics. "If I were you, Jade, I'd shut my mouth before somebody shut it for me." Shaken and afraid, Jade was at loss for words, as she knew, the beast that stood before her, didn't make idle threats. Before long, the other kids realized what was happening, and began to gather around. Meanwhile, the dogs and cats were watching everything from across the street.

* * * *

"Lilly, what are you looking at?" Pierre asked, noticing her gaze. "If I'm not mistaken, there's trouble across the street." she said, looking worried. "Well, I don't see what the big deal is. All I see, are a bunch of kids standing on the corner, waiting for a school-bus." he said. "Pierre, look closely, and you'll notice, the one they call, Rilee is giving Jade a hard time." Lilly said, explaining her concern. "But why would she do that, Lilly? I don't understand." "I don't either, Pierre, but I intend to put a stop to it." Just then, Oliver and Tino approached the gate, with Clyde not far behind. "What's the big fuss?" Clyde asked. Lilly was quick to answer. "There's a big problem across the street." "Let me guess. Is it Rilee again?" Oliver asked. "Yup! It sure is, Ollie. There's gotta be a way we can help Jade." "But how? We're stuck behind this locked gate." Oliver said. Meanwhile, Lilly had been planning her strategy. "One way or another, I'll get this gate open, and when I do, I'll be across the street, faster than any of you can gulp down a cheese-snack." she said, determined to help Jade. "Lilly, have you lost your mind? You know we're not allowed to leave the yard without permission!" Clyde said, looking panicked. "Calm down, boy. Since when, did you became such a rule-geek?" Lilly asked, giving him a look. Meanwhile, Sassy was perched on the window-sill, eavesdropping on the dog's conversation. "Lilly, I'd be careful if I were you. You don't need any trouble." she warned. "I get it, Sassy, but I can't just stand here and watch Rilee pick on Jade." Suddenly, as if on que, the bully began her assault. All watched in horror, as Jade cried out, in pain from stinging slaps to her skin. Rilee continued her malicious attack, before turning her aggression on Jade's backpack, violently, shaking its contents onto the street. Jade watched as her school papers littered the roadway, and were picked up by the breeze. She noticed their gentle glide, as they began to float freely, escaping down the street. Oh, how she longed to be like the paper in the wind, she thought, but her reality was grounded hard against the pavement, utterly bereft of speech, with Rilee, looming over her. "What's the matter, you little twerp? Got nothin to say?" Rilee sneered. Jade knew, that couldn't be further from the truth, but the words caught in her throat. So, she kept silent. "That's what I thought. Just admit it. You're too afraid to fight back." Rilee said, sure she'd made her point. With that, Lilly was even more determined to help. Standing behind the gate, she called out to Jade, but her words carried the sound of barking to the human ear, instantly catching Rilee's attention. She turned to see Lilly, harnessed in her wheel-cart. "Well, would you look at that." she said, mockingly. "The itty-bitty dog needs training wheels." Meanwhile, Jade remained on the pavement, reeling from the recent attack. Pushing herself to her feet, her legs began to wobble, while her trembling hands worked to gather her school-work, that lay spread across the roadway. Entertained by such a sight, Rilee laughed, as Jade continued her paper chase across the street, and up against the fence to where Lilly stood. It was then, the girl and the dog, locked eyes, instantly sharing a mutual understanding. Lilly began to speak. "Jade, I can help, but I need you to unlock the gate and let me out." she said. Again, her words sounded of intense barking, caused Jade to startle. Noticing this, Rilee threw her head back in laughter. "What's the matter, Jade? Are you afraid of the little dog?" she shouted. So reminiscent of her dream, Jade thought, as she knew, the accusation wasn't true. Fueled with adrenaline, Jade stood by the gate, knowing what she had to do. A sly smile spread across her face, as she prepared to do the unthinkable. Raising her hand to the latch just beyond Lilly's reach, Jade pulled open the gate, instantly, freeing the dogs. All at once, they bolted across the street, and converged on Rilee. Full of fear, she instantly, found herself confronted by five little dogs, all bearing teeth, doing their best to look for ferocious. Determined to make their point, Pierre ran circles around Rilee's feet, while Clyde tugged at her pant-legs, causing her to stumble. Oliver came next with old Tino riding him like a racehorse. In an instant, the pint-size poodle, leapt from Ollie's back, and onto Rilee's shoulders, causing her to panic. The kids were in hysterics, as they watched her frantically, try to free herself from the man-eating poodle. After all, everyone knew, Lilly and her friends, were of no real danger. But even still, Rilee was left shaken and afraid, once the dogs backed away. So, with the tables turned, Jade walked up, to the bully, looking her square in the eye. "What's the matter, Rilee? Are you afraid of the little dogs?" she asked, mirroring her mocking tone.

Silence spread across the bus-stop... All watched in horror, unsure of what would happen next, for there was no doubt, the bully would retaliate against her victim's daring act. Alas, Jade's stance was bold and confident, determined to be the victor. Locked in a stare, the girls stood, nose to nose. Jade's breaths were deep, and her legs trembled beneath her, for behind her stern look, was a looming dread. Cognizant of the others gathered around, Jade maintained her confident stare. She uttered not a single word, but her actions spoke volumes, as an emotional liberation took place, freeing her from the daily torment that for too long, broke her spirit. It was do or die, Jade thought. Choosing the former, she continued to look her opponent, directly in the eye, wordlessly, daring her to make another move. For she knew, to challenge Rilee, was to challenge herself. And so, to be triumphant over her fears, would be the ultimate defeat against the bully...

"Come on, Jade. If you think you're so tough, show me what you're made of!" Rilee challenged. "I don't need to prove anything to you." Jade said, maintaining her direct stare. "Just admit it, you're just a chicken." "Rilee, you're the who's afraid, not me. You don't scare me anymore. So, you can take your mean-girl attitude, and get lost!" Listening to herself, Jade could hardly believe her own audacity. "Who are you calling, afraid?" the bully asked. "You, Rilee." Jade answered. Her voice was drenched with an eerie calmness. Puzzled by her victim's sudden show of confidence, Rilee pushed harder to engage Jade in combat. "Do something, you little twerp, or are you gonna just stand there?" "I am doing something." Jade said. Her calm and collected tone spoke volumes, as did her bold stance. No longer would she cower to the bully, as Jade finally realized, the bully had no power of her. But refusing to relent, Rilee made one last attempt to overpower her sufferer. Determined to prove her fearlessness, she charged at Jade, but thinking fast, Jade jumped to one side. Her unexpected maneuver caused Rilee to lose her balance, and fall to the ground. All were in hysterics, as her clumsy stumble was unexpected. Surrounded by the mockery, Rilee remained on the pavement, looking up, at all the laughing faces. She wanted to run and hide, but instead, drowned in the embarrassment of it all. But, Jade took no pride in her bold action, as kindness and compassion, were more her attributes. Leading by example, she reached a hand to Rilee, and helped her to her feet. It was game-over, Rilee thought, as she stood, brushing herself off, knowing all eyes were on her. Jade knew then, she'd made her point. As if on que, the bus arrived and rolled to a stop. The sound of the rumbling engine filled the air, as its tall, bifold doors opened wide. The dogs watched as the students formed a line, and climbed aboard. Jade was last to ascend the steps. Stopping short, she turned, noticing Lilly standing there in her wheel-cart. So reminiscent of her dream, she thought. Contemplating the unthinkable, the idea of sneaking her onto the bus, crossed her mind. Lilly noticed Jade's hesitation, and hoped she might bring her along. Instead, the young girl turned to leave, and disappeared inside the bus.

Before long, Lilly found herself standing on the corner with an ache in her heart, as she watched the bus drive out of sight. Reflecting on the morning's events, she wondered how a child as beautiful as Jade, could take so long to recognize her invaluable self-worth. As it was, Rilee harbored the most feelings of self-doubt, as her abusive actions were likely motivated by a longstanding discontent, buried deep within. Out of concern for Jade, Lilly began to imagine the worrisome possibilities of what might occur once the kids arrived at school. It crossed her mind that Rilee might retaliate against Jade for her recent, bold action, and it concerned her that she wouldn't be around to protect her from future harassment. Meanwhile, Pierre sensed his sister's concern, and offered his best comforting words. "Try not to worry, Lilly. I'm sure, Jade will be just fine. If you remember, the way she stood up for herself, was pretty impressive." he said. Lilly nodded in agreement. "You're right, Pierre. I'm sure it took a lot of courage for her to do that. It's just, I don't think I'll ever forget what I witnessed out here, this morning." "Nor will I, Lilly." he began. "But you have to admit, the look on Rilee's face was priceless, when old Tino here, catapulted onto her shoulders, and wouldn't let go when she tried to shake him off. Now, that's something worth remembering." he said, with a chuckle. Recalling the scene, Lilly smiled to herself despite her worry. "Yeah, that was something else, all right." she said, looking to Tino. Welcoming the praise, the tea-cup size poodle, puffed his chest, feeling larger than life, despite his modest stature. Lilly believed, each of her brothers, exhibited extreme, heroic behavior, when they courageously bolted from the yard in a valiant attempt to protect a bullied child. Indeed, she was proud of them. Conversely, Sassy sat in judgment, watching from the window. She believed the dog's haphazard actions, lacked proper planning. But despite her disapproval, even she agreed, Tino executed his maneuver with adroit skill, when he somersaulted from Oliver's back, and onto Rilee's, easily classifying his daring stunt, a phenomenal gymnastic feat.

Dawning on Clyde, they weren't supposed to leave the yard without permission. "Okay, everyone. I'm glad we put Rilee in her place, but we'd better head home before anyone notices we're missing." he said, looking worried. Oliver nodded in agreement. "He's right, Lilly. Come on, let's go. Besides, the dog-officer might drive by and mistake us for a pack of lost dogs. Rolling her eyes, Lilly was sure, her brothers were overreacting. "Ollie, come on now. You mean to tell me, after everything that's happened out here this morning, you're worried about getting picked up for a leash-law violation?" she asked. "Well, not exactly, Lilly. It's just that our work out here is done, and we should all get home." he explained. Pierre agreed. "He's right, Lilly. Like I told you, I believe that Jade will be okay." he said. "But, what if Rilee starts on her again, once they get to school?" she asked, looking worried. "I understand your concern." Pierre began. "Trust me, neither one of us will forget what we witnessed out here, this morning. Bear in mind though, Jade turned the tables on Rilee, so, I think you can put your worries to rest, Lilly." Nodding her head, she wanted to believe him. "I suppose you're right, Poodle. I just wish I could be sure." Meanwhile, Tino, was taking in everything his worrisome sister said. Turning to Lilly, the old dog offered his wise insight. Although his tone was cracked and weak, his words, rang loud and clear. "Lilly, how can you expect Jade to have faith in herself, if even you, doubt her capabilities?" he asked. Pausing, Lilly digested her elder's wise words. Oliver sensed she might still have doubts "Lilly, just remember, even though we offered a strong presence out here today, it was Jade, who picked herself off the ground, and ultimately stood up to Rilee. So, give her some credit." Finally, giving in to a smile, Lilly agreed, her brothers were right. "Okay, Ollie. You guys win. I'm sure, Jade will be just fine. Although, I still wouldn't mind a trip to school, someday." she said, imagining the possibilities. With that, Oliver laughed. "You at school, Lilly? Only in your dreams." he said. "Now, that'd be a story worth writing about…"

Charity and Support

Here are a couple of suggested charitable groups in South East Asia, geared to helping street-dogs in need like, Lilly and Oliver:

A&N Animals Rescue
facebook.com/AnimalRescuePattaya/
Thailand Adopter Club
facebook.com/ThailandAdopterClub/
Headrock Dogs Rescue
https://headrockdogs.org

Support your local shelters to help dogs like, Pierre, Clyde and Tino.

Photo Credit:
Keith McKearney

About the Author

Born and raised in New England, Heidi McKearney is best known for her passion for all animals, as well as a personal mission to adopt senior rescue dogs, and provide them with a loving home in which to live out their golden years. McKearney's first published work, For the Love of Princess Lilly, is a heartwarming tale of a puppy's harrowing journey, and ultimate rescue from the illegal dog-meat trade of South East Asia. A true story, sure to leave you inspired by the young dog's exceptional bravery, and strong will to beat the odds.

www.ingramcontent.com/pod-product-compliance
Lightning Source LLC
Chambersburg PA
CBHW030344180626
46812CB00007B/2749